A Stormy Travel Thru Time

Mandy Jo

To Lisa & Lauren,
Happy Reading
Mandy Jo

The Book:

Heinrich and Gustav are brothers that want to come to America. They have family that is already settled there. They start their adventure in Antwerp Belgium where they will board the Kroonland ship.

Storms will arise mutliple times while they are traveling.

Where all will they go?

Who all with they meet?

Will they make it to America?

A Stormy Travel Thru Time

by

Mandy Jo

Lulu Publishing

1. Edition, 2022

Lulu Publishing
mandyjo@mandyjo.us

Table of Contents

Chapter 1

It is December of 1903 with snow gently falling, Heinrich and his younger brother, Gustav board the Kroonland ship that is heading to America from Antwerp. They are two German travelers in their 20's journeying across the ocean thinking of hopes and dreams. It feels like time is standing still as they wait on the dock to board. What will they find? Will their expectations be met?

There are many boats of all sizes lining the busy docks. The workers and passengers are hurriedly walking everywhere. All around them are more people waiting to board the ships and say good-bye.

Pieter sits at the entrance to the ship filling out information on all the passengers. Gustav and Heinrich tell him their names, ages, gender, marital status, nationality, occupation, whether they can read and write, if they have a ticket to their final destination and who paid for it. The questioning continues. They must declare how much money they have, if they have been to the United States before including when and where, whether they were in prison and why, last place of residence, where they are going and who they are meeting in America. Finally, they have to state whether they are Anarchists, their mental and physical condition, and if they have deformities or are crippled.

Once their paperwork is in order with all the questions answered, they are able to go on board. The travelers walk around the ship. First they find their room and put all their bags down. They sit on the beds. Heinrich looks at Gustav, "I cannot believe we are on our way to America. This is going to be a fresh start. I have heard that there are opportunities for a man to do whatever he wants to. There is an abundance of jobs. Karl is a miner, and he said that he can get us both hired if we are interested."

There's a knock on the door, and the deep male voice says, "We leave in a few hours. Everyone is expected on deck to wave good-bye to the people on the dock."

"Ok!" They both reply back.

Gustav lays back on his bed, "This is pretty scary, if you think about it. We are heading across an ocean. We cannot see what's ahead. At some point we will be so far out on the water that we will not be able to see any land. We have left everything we know behind and for what? We can go by what Karl has said, but it is still unknown to us."

"Getting kinda philosophical there, are we?" Heinrich chuckles.

"Yeah, it just has me thinking. I've never been this far from home nor have I been out on the ocean before. I am excited and scared."

"I get it. I'm just teasing ya. Let's go walk around. We'll have plenty of time to be in our room when we are out in the middle of the ocean with nothing to see."

They enjoy a walk on the deck where they feel the sun on their faces, while smelling the fresh ocean air. Around the corner they come upon the band that is playing. There is a clarinet player, a French horn, a couple of trombones, a snare drummer, a bass drummer, a mini tuba and four trumpet players. They are playing “Heidelberg.”

“I love that we get music on board here. This will make the trip more enjoyable,” Heinrich says.

Gustav suggests, “Hey, let’s go sit in the lounge for a few minutes. We have a couple hours until we set sail.”

“Great idea. I hear they have some leather armless chairs are quite comfortable. Plus we can get a drink.”

Upon walking into the lounge they find a player sitting at a grand piano. “I think he must be playing his own music. I do not recognize it. What about you Gustav?”

“I do not, but it is enjoyable.”

The guys sit down at a small dark oak table and a waitress walks up, “What can I get you gentlemen to drink?”

“I’ll take a Weihenstephan Hefe Weissbier,” Gustav answers.

Heinrich tells her, “Same for me.”

"I'll be right back with those," she says, then turns and walks over to the bar. The waitress returns a few minutes later with their drinks.

The piano player changes up the music and begins playing Christmas carols with "O' Tannenbaum." They start singing along with the rest of the room, and the merry-making continues through multiple songs.

"Let's go up on deck to look around," Heinrich suggests.

When they arrive up on the top deck, a horn blows letting everyone know that they are setting sail in five minutes. The men run to the sides of the ship to get a prime spot along the railing. They wave to the crowd on the dock. The ship's engines start to move it forward as the waving and cheering continues. Within minutes, they have cleared the marina and are heading towards the open sea.

"I can't believe we are off! Soon we will see Karl. He says that he loves living in Saginaw," Heinrich tells Gustav.

"I believe that Adolf is there as well."

"Yes, they came over together on a ship, The Vaderland, back in April."

"Our first Christmas in America. The trees, the ornaments, the candles. It's so exciting."

"Yes, Gustav, it will be great fun. Plus we will see relatives we haven't seen in a long time."

"That sounds great."

The men continue talking as they walk around the upper deck. They catch up to Anton and Pauline Richter. "Hello! How are the two of you?" Heinrich asks them.

Anton shakes their hands, "We are excited about our new adventure. We are going to Pennsylvania. How about you?"

"We are going to Michigan. This is exciting, we agree."

"I couldn't believe all the questions that we were asked prior to getting on." Gustav says.

Pauline nods her head, "Yes, there were quite a few. I think they know everything there is to know about us."

"Plus they wrote it all down. They are going to get a cramped hand doing all of that for all of these passengers." Heinrich laughs.

Anton replies, "That's going to be a ton of paper and ink. I wonder if someone will create an easier way of recording all the necessary information."

"Like what?" Heinrich questions him with a bewildered look on his face.

"Oh, I have no idea, but I'd love to know."

The group makes their way to the bistro. Sommer greets them, “Willkommen beim Bürgermeister. Ihr vier?”

“Ja Dankeschön.” Heinrich answers.

“Folge mir bitte.” She walks them to a table along the side of the railing, and places the menus in front of them.

Gustav says with a smile, “I am having the Sauerbraten with spätzle.”

“I will also, but I bet it’s not as good as mutter’s.” Heinrich adds.

“This is true.” Gustav agrees and they all nod.

Irene walks up to their table, “May I take your order?”

“I will have the Kartoffel Kloesse.” Pauline orders.

Anton says, “I’ll take the Schweinefleisch und Rotkohl.”

“I’ll have the wurst linsen suppe.” Heinrich tells her.

Finally Gustav orders, “I will have the Sauerbraten mit Spätzle.”

“Danke. I will be back with those shortly.”

Gustav looks at Heinrich, “I thought you were having the same things as me?”

"I changed my mind." He grins at him. They all laugh.

"This is great to be on our way. How long does it take to get to America?"

"Pauline, it will take about 10 days if the weather is good. It could be longer if it gets too rough." Heinrich explains. "I am hoping for some smooth sailing."

The group gets quiet as they enjoy the gentle breeze coming in off the ocean.

Minutes later Irene returns with their orders. "I hope you all enjoy your meals."

The travelers sit quietly at the table while they focus on eating their dinner.

After a while, Gustav breaks the silence, "This was great! It tasted just like home."

"I agree," Anton responds.

Within moments their plates are all empty and Irene stops by to pick them up.

"How about we go for a walk along the deck and look back at the land, while we can still see it?" Pauline asks.

The men all nod in agreement, as they get up and leave the bistro. Their walk takes them along the railing. Looking out at the ocean, Gustav says, “Heinrich, check out those clouds. It's getting dark ahead. Should we all go inside?”

Anton says, “Pauline and I are going inside.” They head for the nearest door.

“Let's stay here and watch the clouds come in.”

The clouds go from a light gray to a dark black color as they are tumbling in faster and faster. There are streaks of lightning and crashes of thunder. The waves are getting higher and higher on the ship.

Heinrich looks at Gustav and says, “Wow, these waves are getting big. I am sure we'll be getting wet very soon.”

“Yeah, maybe we should go inside,” he replies while looking around seeing the other men heading for cover.

“Let's stay outside for a bit longer. I love the adventure. So what if we get a bit wet.”

The ship moves closer to the dark clouds. The lightning is appearing more frequent along with the thunder following each streak. As Heinrich looks around the deck of the boat he is seeing everyone has taken cover. They are alone.

“Ok, let's go inside,” he says to Gustav.

A wave comes up and gets the deck wet, missing them by inches. They change their walking to running. Lightning is striking all around the ship when the entire sky lights up blinding them, a loud thunder cracks deafening them, and the next moment everything goes dark and silent.

Chapter 2

Opening their eyes, blinking a few times and scanning the area around them, something is dramatically different. "This does not look like the same ship. This is much bigger," Heinrich says.

"So, what ship are we on?"

"I have no idea. Let's go find out."

Standing up, getting their balance and then stretching, they slowly walk towards the flags on the boat and turn to see what else is around them. There's writing on the ship and it says, "Edmund Fitzgerald."

"Well, at least that tells us the name of the ship and verifies that we are not on the right ship. How did we get here?" Gustav asks.

Heinrich shakes his head, "I have no idea, but let's continue walking and see if we can find someone."

They come upon a man swabbing the deck. He's about the same age they are but he is built large, like a bodybuilder.

"Excuse us sir, can we ask you a question?" Heinrich asks him.

"Sure."

"What day is it?"

"Saturday."

"Sorry, I meant, what date is it"

"It's November 9th."

"What year?"

The man looks at them with a puzzled face, "1975, why?"

"We had a hard sleep and it felt like we woke up in a different time."

"Ok, I guess." The man went back to his mopping.

"Thank you."

Heinrich and Gustav walk away from the man and make sure that they are out of hearing distance before speaking to each other.

"It looks like we have traveled through time," Heinrich whispers.

"What's up with that and how do we get back?"

"I don't know, but how do we explain how we got here?"

"Let's see if we can figure it out without attracting any attention to ourselves. They will consider us stow aways and we could be sent to the brig."

"Yes, I think that'll be best. That man didn't seem too curious about who we are, so hopefully we can keep it up."

They continue walking on the deck. Reaching a door Gustav pulls it open. Making their way down the hallway, they pass the bosun's stores and find themselves at the recreation room. There is no one inside.

"I guess they are all busy working," Heinrich mentions.

"Yeah, let's go back outside. I think not getting in the way will be our best bet."

Turning around they see someone opening the door. "Chow is in the mess," he yells and shuts the door.

"So, do we go find the mess?" Gustav asks.

Heinrich shrugs his shoulders, "I don't know. He didn't seem phased by us being here. We might as well."

"I am guessing that the mess is not in here. Let's go out and see where everyone is headed to."

Walking outside they see men heading up the stairs, and they follow at the end of the line. As they enter the hallway, the smell of stew comes wafting by them. Gustav and Heinrich look at each other, smile and nod. Proceeding through the line they find themselves in the mess, grab a tray and a bowl of stew is placed on it. They sit down at a table, hoping to blend in.

“I’m John. Your names?”

“I’m Heinrich and this is Gustav.”

“You guys must be working in a different area from myself.”

“Yes, we are,” replied Gustav.

The men continue to finish their stew and get up from the table. “Have a good day,” John says.

“Good day,” they both respond.

They place their trays in the bin and walk out the door. Once they are downstairs and along the railing, they stop and look at each other with a sigh of relief.

Heinrich says, “Can you believe we were able to get food and eat without any hassle?”

“It surprised me. I thought for sure the conversation was going to go in a different direction.”

“Yes, I think we need to continue to stay low profile though. The fewer questions, the better.”

"Let's get moving though. If we are not in one spot too long, hopefully we can remain unnoticed until we can get off this ship, wherever it is going."

"I like that plan."

They continue walking along the railing from the stern to the bow. John comes up to them, "How would you guys like to join us in the recreation room to play some cards?"

"We would like that. What time?" Heinrich replies.

"Being that a bunch of us are off, we are headed there now." The three men turn and go to meet the other guys to play cards.

Upon entering the recreation room, they are greeted, "Come, sit, we are playing Pinochle. Do you know how to play?" Sam asks.

"Yes, we have played before." Heinrich answers.

John replies, "Great! Heinrich, you will be partners with Sam and I will be partners with Gustav."

The tables around them have groups of four men playing cards. Time goes by quickly and the door opens, "Alright men, get back to work."

Everyone gets up and leaves immediately. Heinrich and Gustav follow the men outside. They walk over to the railing away from the group.

“That was fun, and I am glad that they didn’t ask any questions about us. Now where to?” Gustav asks.

“Yes, it was. I don’t know. I guess we can walk along the railing. No one has questioned us being here, so far.”

The men stood along the railing watching out over the water. “I wonder where we are. I’ve never heard of the Edmund Fitzgerald.”

The wind is starting to pick back up and the waves are rolling up the side of the ship. Heinrich looks to the sky and watches as the clouds are getting bigger, darker and closer to them.

“Here we go again, something is about to happen. Check out those clouds,” he says to Gustav.

“Yep, that’s what it looked like last time. At least we know what’s going to happen. The only question is, where will we end up next? Back on the Kroonland? In America?”

Holding onto the railing they brace themselves for the impact. The waves are cresting to heights greater than the ship, tossing it up and down. It starts to rain, with lightning streaking across the clouds. Once again, there’s a bright light with a crash of thunder and then darkness and silence.

Chapter 3

They look around and then at each other. "Where are we?" asks Gustav.

"I have no idea. This does not look like a ship."

"I would say not, but at least we are on dry ground and the storm is over."

Flying overhead is an airplane. The body of it is white with a red and blue tail. Gustav points up to it and looks at Heinrich, "What's that?"

"I heard that Wilbur and Orville Wright had been working on a flying machine. I don't remember it looking like that though."

They stand up and walk on the boardwalk up to the lighthouse. The sun is shining through the white fluffy clouds. Under their feet the water laps on the rocks. Scanning every direction as they walk looking to see if there is anyone around.

Arriving at the lighthouse entrance they knock, wait a few seconds, and try again. "Looks like no one is here. We will have to continue on. Let's follow that path and see where it goes," Heinrich says.

Continuing on down the snowy path they see no one. “This is beyond strange. How are we the only ones around?” Gustav asks.

“I don’t know but we will just keep walking until we find someone. I am sure it will happen eventually.”

Walking along they see many prints and some strange tracks. “I wonder what made those. They look bumpy and go for a long way,” Heinrich says.

“Yeah, I have never seen that before.”

Continuing along the path they arrive at a plowed road. Although it is cleared there are no vehicles nor people in view in either direction. There is a light snow in the air and it melts instantly on the asphalt.

“Which way do you want to go?” Gustav asks.

“How about we head to the right? It should put us back along the water.”

They get to the hairpin turn in the road and still see no signs of life. A rabbit hops out from the brush next to them.

“Hey, a rabbit,” Gustav says quietly.

“Why are you whispering? We are the only ones here.”

“That’s true, but I didn’t want to scare the rabbit. At least it’s some form of life.”

"Yeah, this is strange not to see any people. I wonder where we are. All we know so far is that we were on a boardwalk by a lighthouse and now we are on a road by the water. This looks like the ocean, you can't see any land around it."

Walking along the road by the water they come up to a sign that says, "Lake Michigan Circle Tour."

"Ok, it looks like we made it to America and even Michigan. Do you know how close Lake Michigan is to Saginaw?" Gustav asks.

"I don't think it is real close because they never mention it."

"So, we'll have to keep going to see where in Michigan we are."

"Agreed. I hope Saginaw is not too far away. Plus, we need to figure out what year it is."

As the time travelers continue to follow the road it leads them away from the water. They see a two-story white house in the distance. Picking up their pace they make their way to to its front door.

"Ok, let's go up to the door and see if anyone is home," Heinrich says. Gustav nods in agreement.

The pair walk up the shoveled driveway and sidewalk They step onto the front porch which has been cleared of snow, too.

Heinrich knocks on the door. They wait there patiently. No one answers.

“Really, no one home? This is just crazy,” Gustav comments.

“Well, let’s continue on and see where the next house is and if anyone is home.”

It is quiet with the exception of the waves crashing on the shore behind them. They arrive at a long winding driveway that goes into the trees.

“Should we venture back?” Heinrich questions.

“Yeah, why not? It certainly can’t hurt.”

“Let’s go.”

The pair walk down the snowy driveway making sure to stay in the tire tracks. The trees clear, and they see a couple of red Chevrolet pickup trucks sitting out front and all covered in snow. Walking up the stairs they knock on the dark wood doors.

They wait a few minutes and turn around to walk away when there’s a voice that says, “How can we help you?”

Looking all around, they see no one but each other. The voice says again, “How can we help you?”

There's a pause and the voice speaks again, "Turn around and come up to the door. Face the door and you'll see the small hole in it. This is a camera."

They go up to the door and face the small hole. "We are lost and don't know where we are.."

"You are in Ludington, Michigan. Where are you headed?"

"Saginaw, Michigan. We don't know which direction to go in."

"I'll be right out to help you. Give me a couple minutes."

They step away from the door and look at each other, "This is the most bizarre thing I have ever seen. The door was talking to us. Do we stay?" Heinrich asks.

"Sure, why not? What do we have to lose?"

The door opens and a tall, thin Caucasian man appears in the doorway. "Welcome, come on in." They follow him inside the house.

"My name is William Robinson. You guys?"

"I am Heinrich and this is Gustav."

"Those sound like very German names. Plus, the accent. I didn't see a vehicle. How did you get here?"

"Yes, we are from Germany. That's a great question. Let me ask you a question. What do you think about time travel?"

William looks at them with a confused face, “Well, honestly, I haven’t thought about it. I don’t have an opinion on it. Why?”

“Well, we are trying to figure out what the date is,” Gustav tells him.

“It is December 5th, 2001. Why? What date did you leave and expect to arrive?”

“See, that’s the thing. We’re not sure that you will believe us,” Heinrich replies.

“That’s ok. I will believe just about anything. This has been a weird year.”

Heinrich continues, “Ok, we started out heading for America on the SS Kroonland.”

“What date was that?”

“December 4th, 1903,” Gustav replies.

“Let me do the math on that one. That’s ninety-eight years ago. You don’t look that old. How did you end up here?”

“That is what we are trying to figure out. We boarded the Kroonland, got into a storm and ended up on the Edmund Fitzgerald. Then another storm came along and we ended up by the lighthouse and walked here,” Heinrich explains.

“The common occurrence then is the storm. I don’t believe we are supposed to get one today. Just some lake effect snow. Let’s go to the backroom. We can see what’s going on outside.” They follow him through the house and into the room with a wall of glass windows.

“Wow, what a great view!” Gustav says.

“Yes, I really enjoy it. From here we can watch what’s going on with the weather. I do this on a regular basis.”

Margaret walks into the room. “Hello! William, you didn’t tell me we had company.”

“That’s because you were busy working. These gentlemen have traveled quite a distance. This is Heinrich and Gustav. They are from Germany and are headed to Saginaw.”

“Glad to meet you both. How did you end up here? I don’t think we are in between those two locations.” She asks them.

Heinrich answers, “It is a different story. We have been traveling in a rare form of transportation.”

“Ok, you have me curious. What kind is that? I didn’t hear any vehicles pull up.”

Gustav smiles and replies, “We have traveled by storm. Every time there is a storm it appears that we go from location and time to another location and distant time.”

“So you are time travelers. I have read many books on it. You two are my first real encounters though. This is interesting. William, are we able to pull anything up on that computer about where they have been?”

William walks to his desk and sits down. “Come on over here and we will see what comes up. I believe I have found some things before on here about Germany.”

They all gather around him with Heinrich seated next to William. He turns the machine and monitor on. “This is an interesting thing. What is it and what’s it do?” Gustav asks.

“This is a computer and this is the monitor. The computer is where things happen and the monitor is where we can see what is happening. This has an operating system called Windows XP. With this we can get information from all over the globe. These buttons are called a keyboard and that is called a mouse. A lot has been invented since the two of you boarded the Kroonland.” William explains. “I am sure that you have a lot of questions, but let me ask you some. Where are you guys going?”

“We are headed to Saginaw, Michigan to see our cousins Karl Kaldener and Adolf Rheinhold.” Heinrich answers.

“Ok, let me do a search on Karl and see what comes up. There’s not a whole lot on him, except that he came over with Adolf and they were going to see Albert Schlegel.”

Margaret asks, "How about we have something to eat. I have some cabbage rolls in the slow cooker and they should be ready. I can pair them with some mashed potatoes."

"Thanks. We'll do that." William replies. The group goes out to the dining room. "I am glad to have you two as our dinner guests. It will be interesting to see what we can find on the internet."

Heinrich says, "Thanks. We are glad that you welcomed us. We couldn't believe how quiet it was and that there was no one around."

"Yes, this time of year it is quiet. It is much busier in the summer. At night though we have the best Christmas lights. I hope you are here to see them." Margaret tells them.

The room becomes quiet while the group eats for the next twenty minutes. Margaret breaks the silence, "Well, I must have made a good meal with how everyone got quiet. I am glad that you all enjoyed it. I'll clean up the dishes while you all get back to figuring this time travel stuff out."

William, Heinrich, and Gustav get up from the table and go back over by the computer. "I can search for information on Adolf."

"What is the internet? You had mentioned it." Gustav asks.

"It's where everything is stored. You connect remotely to a type of library and it gives you all kinds of information. When it first came out, they called it the information superhighway. I have been able to fill in a lot of my family tree from searching on it. We've been here in the United States for quite some time."

Heinrich says, "Can you show me where we are compared to where Saginaw is? Information like that?"

"Yes, there is a place I can go to map it out. Let me show you."

He brings up MapQuest, enters in his address and then Saginaw. "You see, it shows that it's about 2 hours and 40 minutes. So, you are close, but not close enough to walk."

"Yeah, I would say that we are not walking it. Also, would Karl or Adolf even be around anymore? It puts them at being over a hundred years old." Heinrich asks.

"I doubt they are around. I am sure their family still is. However, they wouldn't live in the same house."

Gustav scratches at his chin, "This is really hard to understand. I know where we've been and I know the dates that everyone has told us, but I don't know how we have actually gone from one place to another and one time to another. It's just really crazy."

"Yes, I can understand what you are saying. Let's go outside. It's a great view."

They walk outside, sit down, and watch as the skies start to darken. The snow begins to fall as time goes by and blankets the ground and trees. The winds pick up and the snow is blowing all around. Lightning bolts streak across the sky. Thunder begins to crash a few minutes after each occurrence. It keeps getting closer together.

"This storm is really picking up more and more. If ya'll get transported to another time and place, it was great to meet you guys."

"Thanks for the hospitality," Heinrich responds.

The next lightning strike is followed by a loud crack that lasts a few moments, and it goes completely black and silent.

Margaret walks out to the deck, "A storm came in and they are gone?"

William nods his head, she sits down, and they watch the sky.

"I hope they make it to their destination ok." She says.

Chapter 4

Rubbing their eyes and opening them, they look at each other. "We have transported once again. I wonder where we are now." Gustav questions.

"Let's go see where we are now."

Getting up off the ground they brush the snow off and walk down the gravel driveway. "Hey, there's a castle, let's go in there," Heinrich suggests.

"Hopefully someone is there," Gustav replies.

They arrive at the castle, "Hey, the drawbridge is down. That's a good sign!" Heinrich comments.

Walking across the bridge to the front doors of the castle they wait patiently and look around without moving from the entrance. All they see are snow covered trees with another castle type structure in the distance.

The door begins to open inward and a voice from behind it says, "Can I help you?"

"Yes, we are lost and not sure where we are," Heinrich answers him.

The door opens further, “Please come in. You are at the Rochester Castle.”

Gustav and Heinrich walk inside and look around at all the stone work. It’s a gorgeous castle, but so many questions are going through their heads.

“Where is Rochester Castle?” Heinrich asks.

“It’s in the Metro Detroit area.”

“Where?” they both question.

“Let me ask you guys, where are you from?”

“Germany. I am from Wickede and he’s from Altona,” Heinrich answers.

“You guys are a long way from home.”

“Yes, although, you have no idea how far.”

“Where are you headed?”

“We are both headed to Saginaw, Michigan.” Gustav replies.

“You aren’t too far off. We are about an hour or so south of there, but you are in the correct state,” he tells them. “Let’s get you something to eat and then figure out how to get you to Saginaw. My name is Burchard.”

“This is Gustav and I am Heinrich. Thank you for welcoming us into your home.”

As they follow Burchard through the castle hallway they notice all the intricate woodwork. He leads them by another door, and they go down a set of green plaid carpeted stairs that have stone walls on both sides. They arrive in a fully finished basement with a bar. There’s a figurehead of a woman on the right side of the bar.

“Have a seat. Would you like something to drink?” Burchard asks.

Gustav replies, “Do you have Weihenstephan Hefe Weissbier?”

“Let me see what we have in the cellar. I’ll be right back,” he says as he goes to the stairway behind the bar.

Heinrich turns and looks at Gustav and says, “I’ll be surprised if they have it. Plus, interesting that he has not asked more questions or that is coming shortly.”

“Yeah, I am sure when he comes back he will have more questions for us. How’s he going to react to time travel?”

They sit in the burgundy leather bar stools and look about the room. There’s a metal blimp hanging from the stucco ceiling and a train track around the top of the room and a miniature wooden rocking horse in the corner.

"This place is really cool. I feel like we are back in Germany," Heinrich remarks.

Burchard comes back up into the bar area with a case in hand. "I found some. Would you like them in mugs, glasses or just the bottle?"

"We will take the beer in mugs. Thanks," Gustav replies.

He pours them and slides them across the bar. "So, you guys are from Germany. How long have you been here in the US? Are you here on holiday, work or do you live here now?"

"That's an interesting story and I'm not sure you will believe us. We started out on one ship that was headed to America, ended up in a storm, then onto another ship, another storm came up and we landed at a lighthouse. This last storm landed us here at your home. We are trying to figure out the whole who, what, where, why and how," Heinrich tells him.

"Ok, that's an interesting story. Very creative, I'll give you that."

Gustav adds in, "Yes, we didn't figure that you'd believe us. It's been an interesting day."

"Say I believe you guys. What year was it when you got on the first ship? What was the ship?"

"It was 1903 and we were on the Kroonland headed for America," Heinrich answers.

“Woa, wait a minute. You guys are from 1903? That’s so incredible.”

“Yes, we did not make it all the way across the ocean on that ship. There was a big storm and the next thing we knew we were on another ship. It was the Edmund Fitzgerald and the year was 1975,” Gustav tells him.

“How did you get from one ship to another?”

Heinrich replies, “We don’t know. I haven’t figured it out yet. There was a violent storm with high winds, lots of lightning. Then, poof, we open our eyes and we are on the other ship at another time. Not only do I not know how we got from one ship to the other, but I also don’t know how we traveled ahead almost 72 years.”

“Good thing you got off the Edmund Fitzgerald ship, it sank and took all the lives of those on board.”

“We were in that storm. It was crazy, the storm came up just like the first ship and the next thing we know we are next to a lighthouse. We went to a house and found out we had landed on December 5th, 2001. We met a nice couple that fed us dinner.” Gustav explains.

“So, now you end up here. It’s December 15th, 2028. Quite the jump from where you started to now. You’re looking at a hundred and twenty-five years.”

Heinrich shakes his head, “I have no idea what’s up with this. I also don’t know how we get back to 1903. Do you have any ideas?”

“No, I have no ideas. Although Johann, the owner of this great castle, has a fascination with time travel. He is expected to be back shortly. So, relax and enjoy your beer.”

The guys sit back, take a deep breath and drink their beer. The basement gives off an oak smell that is coming from the fireplace. Burchard turns on the sound system and selects “Tell Me Pretty Maiden,” which was a hit in 1902.

“Wow! I love that you have this music and beer. It really makes me feel like I am at home in Germany,” Gustav says as he’s tapping his fingers on the bar and drinking.

Johann walks up behind them, “Hi guys! I am so glad that you could join us. Sounds like you have come a long way. I’d love to hear more. I have some friends stopping by. We’ll go upstairs to the dining room. Follow me.” He motions them toward the stairs.

When they get upstairs, they walk through the front entryway by the winding wood staircase with red carpeted steps. The knight in shining armor is guarding the front doorway. Bright and twinkling chandeliers are all over the main floor ceiling. Making their way into the dining room, Burchard says, “Please have a seat. Some more friends will be joining us in a moment.”

The doorbell rings, “Excuse me, I’ll be right back.” Burchard goes to the front door. They can hear him at a distance, “Welcome! Come right in. We are in the dining room.”

The crew joins them and the travelers stand up. Johann introduces everyone, “This is Kat, Eddie, Carl, Anna, and AJ, and Vicki. Gang, this is Heinrich and Gustav. Everyone, please have a seat.” He sits and explains, “Ok, these guys have a great story. You know my fascination with time travel. Well, I think we are witnessing it in real life right now. I will have Heinrich explain their journey so I don’t miss anything.”

“Thanks Johann. You have made us feel welcome, and we are grateful. I’ll give you the abbreviated version. We started this journey December 4th, 1903 in Antwerp, Belgium. We were on board the SS Kroonland that was bound for America. A big storm came up with high waves, thunder and lightning. Suddenly we were transported to another ship. It was the Edmund Fitzgerald on November 9th, 1975. Once again a big storm came up, and we were transported to a lighthouse. We were able to find a nice couple at home. They fed us dinner and tried to help orient us to our location. It was on December 5th, 2001. Then another storm and we were transported here today. How did all these transports happen? We have no idea. The only thing in common was the storm.”

Kat questions, “Ok, so we have all these transports during storms. Are we expecting any storms? It is December in Michigan.”

“Well, anything is possible, but I don’t think so,” Carl answers.

Eddie asks, “What can we do?”

“I think that I will let them stay here. I have plenty of rooms. It’s just Burchard and myself in this place. We’d love the company. Plus, we can figure out how to get you guys back to 1903.”

“Thanks everyone. We weren’t sure what kind of greeting we would get. So far we have had friendly encounters. The last couple shared their dinner with us. The men on the Edmund Fitzgerald gave us a meal and we played Pinocle with a few of the crew.” Gustav adds.

“Well, no worries here with us. We love to travel, but have never time traveled. There’s a lot of things that have advanced since 1903. You will be amazed and hopefully it’ll help with how to get you back. Where were you headed again?” asks Johann.

Heinrich replies, “We were headed to Saginaw, Michigan to meet up with family. That is, once we landed at Ellis Island and got through the paperwork.”

“Where do we start with getting them up to date, but not overwhelmed?” Anna questions.

Eddie chuckles and answers, “Well, let’s start off with the laptop and show them the website about Ellis Island.”

“Yes, great place to start,” Burchard hands Johann his Microsoft Surface Pro 13. “Thank you. This is a laptop and a tablet computer. This contains all kinds of information and even connects to what we call the internet. This is a virtual world where information is held and everyone can share it. Ellis Island has put all of their papers on what is called a website. This is where the information is at. It's like a virtual address."

He turns it on and faces it toward Gustav and Heinrich showing them how he gets to the page. Then he asks, "Heinrich, what's your last name?"

"Rindhage, you spell it, R, I, N, D, H, A, G, E."

"Great," he types it in as Heinrich spells it for him. "Look, your name comes right up. It shows that you were on the SS Kroonland that sailed on December 4, 1903. It also shows you are 28 years old and that you are married. Also, it has a picture of the paperwork. You were on line number 0014. So, if you were 28 in 1903, that means you would now be 153 now. Just a few years down the road. You guys look great."

"That is crazy that we are this many years down the road. This place looks like what we had at home in Germany. It's very common to see castles similar to yours." Gustav mentions.

Carl says, "Yes, I have seen many pictures of the castles in Germany. In the United States this active castle is a rare find. We have some very modern houses just down the road."

"This is true, I managed to do very well and got this place for a great deal. I have no idea what I am going to do with it."

Burchard mentions, "It's getting close to lunch time and we should be expecting Mark soon."

"I love when Mark comes over with his catering. He does a great job on the food. What are we getting this time?" Eddie asks.

"I ordered some chicken and ribs along with roasted potatoes and bread sticks."

"Great job, Burchard. My favorite things. I hope that you guys will enjoy it as well," Johann says.

There's a knock and Burchard goes to answer it. Opening the door, "Hi Mark! Great to see you."

"Thanks. I have some trays of food for you all."

He walks in and wheels a cart with the trays of food on it. "Hi everyone!" as he gets into the dining room. "I hope everyone is hungry. This is a great feast. I put the barbecue sauce on the side to dip the ribs in if you like. The chicken has a garlic and herb seasoning on it. The potatoes are roasted and the last pan has the breadsticks in it. I hope you all enjoy!"

"Mark, please join us. We have an empty seat," Johann invites him.

"Thanks, but I need to get going. I have another delivery to make." He places the trays in their racks on the buffet and leaves with his cart.

"Let's get some food while it's hot. Our guests can start first."

Heinrich and Gustav get in line for the buffet and the rest follow behind them with Burchard at the tail end. Everyone grabs a stoneware plate, pile mounds of food.

Chapter 5

About 15 minutes later, Johann says, "I hope you all enjoyed lunch." They all nod their heads in approval. "Awesome. I love when Burchard gets Mark to bring in food for us. It's always the best. It's no wonder that he caters for major companies and sports teams. Let's get back to Heinrich and Gustav with how their journey has been and what we can do to help them back to 1903."

Burchard gets up, clears the table and brings in the Microsoft Surface Hub. Johann stands up next to it, "Ok, this is a great board where we can see everything in a much bigger picture. I am going to bring up a Google Doc so that we can create a time line and what all happened."

"Ok, so we began our journey on December 4, 1903 on the SS Kroonland in Antwerp, Germany," Heinrich tells Johann, and he writes it on the board.

"Next, we were waiting for everyone to board. The departure horns finally blew loudly. We waved at the people on the dock as the ship pulled out." Heinrich waits for Johann to write it out before continuing on.

"We are far enough out in the ocean that we cannot see land and a storm starts up. The waves keep getting higher and finally some water comes on the deck. Meanwhile, there is thunder and lightning all around. There's a bright light, a loud crash of thunder and then everything goes dark." He pauses again.

Gustav picks up after Johann has it written out, "We open our eyes, and we are on a ship that we don't recognize. Looking around we see the ship's name in large letters, "Edmund Fitzgerald.""

After a brief pause Heinrich says, "We see someone swabbing the deck, so we ask him what date it is and he tells us that it's November 9th, 1975. Another storm starts up a short time later with the high waves, thunder and lightning. So, it's just like the first one just on a different ship on a different date." He takes a brief break and continues, "Once again we get the bright light and loud crash just before it goes completely dark and silent. We open our eyes and we are on a boardwalk by a lighthouse."

"This is a great story so far. However, I am not understanding the transport part. You aren't physically in anything but just on a ship and then a boardwalk," Carl comments.

Gustav replies, "That's what we don't know either. It's been a crazy day for us, but yet, we have traveled a long way both in time and distance. Where are we?"

"You are right here," Eddie answers, using his right hand as the map of lower, he points to his thumb pad. The group chuckles as Gustav and Heinrich look at him with a questioning look on both their faces.

Carl pipes in, "Ok, let me explain what he was trying to say. Here in Michigan because the state is in the shape of a mitten or a hand, we point on our hand where we are in the state. Locals understand it. Saginaw, where you are planning to go to, is further up towards the crease between the finger and thumb." He points to it on his hand.

"I see, very interesting and portable," Heinrich says with a smile. "After being at the lighthouse, we did go for quite a walk and were finally able to find someone. The lighthouse was in Ludington, Michigan, if you know where that is. Then the next storm rolled in with dark clouds, wind, thunder and lightning. Once again it went super bright and loud to pitch black and silent. Upon opening our eyes we were out in front of this place. We knocked on the door and here we are."

"So, I have this all written up here. The crazy part is, like Carl mentioned, there's no real method of transport. In a movie back in the 1980's and 90's they used a car to physically transport from one time to another. There was another show that used beams and one that used a worm hole. This is using a storm?" Johann asks.

Kat answers, "Yeah, it seems to be the mode of transportation. Kinda different, but hey, it seems to work. The question is, when is the next storm supposed to hit?"

Johann points to the board, "Ok, so we have everything here. Let me bring up some pictures to go with all of this. Here's a picture of the Kroonland. This one is of the Edmund Fitzgerald. Next, we have a couple of pictures of lighthouses in Ludington. Which one looks like the one you guys were at?"

"The top one looks like it," Heinrich replies.

Johann deletes the other one, "Ok, now these are the pictures of everywhere that you have been, with the exception of the house you walked to and this one. Let me bring up the map of Ludington here. We'll try to see where the house is at."

"Wow, this is incredible. That board contains all that stuff?" Gustav asks.

"Yes it does. It's connected to what is called the internet. This is like a library but you can pull the information up from just about anywhere. It's awesome," Johann explains. "We'll look right here. This is the Big Sable Lighthouse, which is the picture that you chose."

Heinrich questions, "Interesting. How close are you going to be able to get to the house?"

"I love this part. You can actually see the front of the house. The pictures are taken using a camera that is posted on top of a vehicle that drives down the road and takes them in a complete 360 degree format," Carl adds in.

Kat asks, "Which direction did you go from the lighthouse?"

"We followed the path and ended up on a road. The road ended up curving to the left where we found one house and no one was home. The next house was on the right side of the road behind some trees. Will this be able to find the house behind the trees?" Gustav replies.

Johann moves the map to the curve on the road south of the lighthouse. "Let's start here. I can change it to street level."

"Wow! That is exactly what we saw. I can't believe it. This is magical," Heinrich says excitedly.

"Yes, that house on the left is the first one we stopped at. Then we kept walking towards those trees."

Moving the map forward he asks, "Ok, now that we are in the trees, which driveway did you go down?"

"We took that first one on the right."

Johann switches the map to the 3D model. The time travelers look at each other and say, "That's the house!"

Snipping a screenshot Johann places a picture in the time line. "This is great. We have your complete journey thus far. The only thing we don't know is why the storms come along and you get transported to a new location and you keep going further in time from where you started. I am not sure how we get you to go back to when you began."

The room is silent for a few minutes while everyone is thinking.

Carl breaks the silence, "Now we need to look at weather patterns on the dates they have mentioned. Also, we should look up on Ellis Island about the ship and ship manifests. It will show when they landed. This will also show us when they get back."

"Yes, let's look up Ellis Island first. I like positive stuff," AJ chimes in.

Johann brings up Ellis Island on the board, "Hey, there's a passenger search. Let's look up your names to see when you arrived."

He enters in their last name, "Look, you both show up and it says you arrived in 1903 on the Kroonland. I can click on your name, passenger record, ship image or ship manifest. This is awesome."

"That's great. We make it to Ellis Island in the same year we left. Now we just have to figure out how to get back to 1903," Gustav says.

Switching to the weather station's website he looks up the forecast for the week, "It looks like we have great weather through Christmas. I know that people will be happy, but that also means no storms. So, I am not sure how and when we can get you back to 1903."

Gustav and Heinrich look at each with distress and puzzlement. Turning to the board that shows a weather forecast that they would normally like Heinrich says, "Well, I guess we are going to have to figure out what to do and where to stay while we wait for another storm or solution."

Johann turns to Burchard and asks, “Can you get two of the rooms ready for our guests?”

“Yes, it would be my pleasure,” He walks out of the room.

Kat stands up, “You know, this to me is very peculiar. There didn’t seem to be any signs of a storm before it appeared. When it was needed, it formed. You know, like a mode of transportation. The question is, do we wait for it to appear or do we make it appear?”

“If you can figure out a way to make it appear, go for it.” Carl responds.

The crew sits looking at the board with the pictures and websites on it. The room grows silent.

Burchard walks quietly in, and says, “All set.” They are startled and he laughs.

“Nice Burchard,” Johann smirks. “Let’s show them to their rooms.” The group gets up and with Burchard in the lead as they ascend the stairs to the hall with the bedrooms.

He opens the door to the first room, “This one is for Heinrich. I hope that you like it.”

Walking into the room, Heinrich thinks to himself, “Wow! This is quite the room. This guy is rich. I wonder if my family lives this way.” Then he says, “I like it. Thank you.”

The rest continue to the room next door, "Gustav, this is for you. I hope you like it." He steps inside and looks around, "This is wonderful. Thank you."

Johann leads the group downstairs, "Are the rest of you staying as well?"

"Yes, we have to see what happens. We need to be here in person." Carl answers.

AJ smiles, "Yep, I am nosey. I admit it. This is just beyond cool. I can't wait to see how this plays out."

The group sits down in the library. The lights go dim. The wind picks up with some tree branches banging on the windows. A loud crack of thunder deafens them and a bright light blinds them.

A few moments later the room is still silent, and Eddie speaks up, "I think we should go check on them. That was just what they have been telling us gets them from one spot to the next."

"Yes, follow me." Johann motions, and they all walk up the stairs to the rooms. The doors are closed. He opens the first one, "Hey Heinrich, are you in here?"

There is no answer and the room is dark. Johann turns on the light and it's empty. Heinrich is nowhere in sight. They continue to the next door.

"Hey Gustav, are you here?" Johann asks while knocking.

Once again, there is no answer. He opens the door, and walks into the room. It, too, is empty.

“Well gang, it looks like Heinrich and Gustav are gone. We can only hope that they have made it back to 1903 this time. We do know that at some point they do, because it’s written on the ship manifest.” Johann tells them.

AJ says sadly, “What a bummer. I was hoping they were going to be around for longer. They did not get their questions answered.”

“Yeah, I wonder where they ended up?” Carl questions.

Chapter 6

The tall old trees by the river bank are swaying in the wind. Heinrich and Gustav open their eyes and sit up in the grass. They look around to see a wooden bridge.

“I don’t know where we are now, but I like the bridge.” Heinrich says.

Gustav nods, “I agree. Check out the big building behind us. Did we go back to Germany? Look across the river.”

“It does look like it. Let’s go walk around and see if we got back to Germany.”

The two men stand up and walk to the bridge. Stopping beside the road, they smile at each other and Heinrich says, “Holz Brücke, wooden bridge. I wonder what this Frankenmuth Bavarian Inn is. Also, it says 1979. So, I would say we have not gone back to our time. If we were in Germany, it wouldn’t have the English underneath it.”

Several vehicles drive past them, the men watch, and Gustav nods, “These vehicles look different from ones we’ve seen before. What year do you think it is?”

“Let’s keep walking and find out. How about going to that building over there. It looks like a huge lodge.”

Heinrich opens the door, and they are greeted, “Welcome to the Bavarian Inn Lodge. I am Jakob. How can I help you?”

“We came into town, but missed a sign. What’s the name of your town?” He questions.

Jakob answers, “This is Frankenmuth. Do you need a room?”

“No, we are just passing through. Thanks!” Gustav replies.

“Ok, you can walk around the lodge if you like.”

Heinrich says, “Thank you. We will go take a walk.”

The men walk towards the hallway, when they hear a familiar voice. “Heinrich and Gustav, is that you guys?”

Spinning around Heinrich replies, “Johann! Yes, it’s us! It’s great to see you.”

“We are up here for a festival and fun. Let’s sit for a moment.” He motions to the high back burgundy chairs and matching couch. “I am glad that you are here. We wondered what happened to the two of you and where you ended up. It is now December 3rd, 2035.”

“Ok, we are being transported further ahead in time. How do we go back in time?” Gustav asks.

Johann shakes his head, “I don’t know. When you guys left us last time, we had no warning and we were not scheduled for weather that would bring a storm with thunder and lightning.

Unfortunately we didn't figure out how you appeared or left. The fortunate part is that you have landed in Frankenmuth, which is a very German area and also very festive, especially for Christmas. Frankenmuth is known for having Christmas all year long."

Kat walks up, "Hi Gustav and Heinrich! Great to see you both here. This is a fabulous town to visit. We come here all the time."

"The decor reminds me of home. Is the whole town like this place?" Gustav asks.

Kat replies, "Yes it is. Plus, with all the great decorations this time of year, one can't help but be excited for Christmas."

"We have to figure out how to get you guys to go back in time, because every time you travel, you've been going further and further from where you started." Johann shares his thoughts.

Eddie walks up to the four along with AJ and sits down. "Hey, nice to see you guys again. Did you guys go somewhere else since we last saw you?"

"No, this was our next stop. I have noticed that we are primarily in the month of December, which is great because I do love Christmas. The decorations here are the best. However, Johann is correct, we keep moving further from when we started. How do we get back? We know that we do get back because we saw it in the ship's manifest." Heinrich adds.

The friends sit quietly and think about what to do next. All of a sudden a group of carolers burst through the front doors singing “O’ Christmas Tree” with the German lyrics included. Heinrich and Gustav join in and the rest of the group quickly chimes in. When they finish the song, the carolers continue walking through the hotel.

“That was fabulous! I can’t believe they had the German lyrics.” Heinrich comments.

AJ adds, “This town is very much a Bavarian town. They call it, Little Bavaria. We come here quite often for festivals and food.”

“Plus, it’s a great place to get in some walking. They just added a nice little walk along the river. If we get here early we can get in a great workout right in town with the hill.

It’s nice to chat about the town, but what are we going to do to get you guys back to where you started?

We have a very large suite and everyone can come up and we’ll get the computer out. It’s time to get to work. Come on everyone!” Johann tells them. The group follows his lead up to the suite by getting into the elevator.

“Interesting, I don’t think we’ve been in an elevator this nice.” Gustav tells them. The group laughs and exits after the door opens.

Everyone exits into the suite, as the elevator is a private one. “Wow! This is huge. Our room on the ship was only about a quarter of this size. Of course, they were expecting us to only sleep there." Heinrich comments.

Johann turns on his Microsoft Surface Pro 17 with its dual monitors. "Now, let's look up time travel via storms and see what appears."

"You're funny Johann," AJ laughs.

"You think I'm funny, but I just found something. Look here, it says that time travel via storms is a fairly common occurrence. Well, that's pretty cool. There are others out there. Scanning this article, it also says that most travelers will experience a minimum of six jumps in time. Although, they are not all going further out. Some have reported that they went back and forth to various times. While others have said that they went further and further." He turns to them, "I am guessing that this means you have at least two more stops. Your first stop was in 1975, the second in 2001, the third in 2028, and this one in 2035. The first one was the only stop not in December."

Kat interjects, "This means they are Christmas time travelers. That's pretty cool. Plus, they landed in the most Christmassy town they could ever end up in. Frankenmuth is perfect. I wonder if their next stops will be further out or if they will go back in time?"

"Does it say if there is a way to predict any of it?" Heinrich questions.

Shrugging his shoulders, Johann turns back to his computer and continues to read, "It says that the travelers did nothing and so far they haven't figured out how to control it or predict it. When the storms appear people are moved through time to various areas. There's a list of names with their dates and locations that they went. Let's see if you guys made the list."

It feels like a forever pause when AJ breaks the silence, "Ok, so tell us, are they on the list? Do we recognize any other names? You're killing us here."

"No, their names are not on the list. However, this list looks to have been started only a couple of years ago by the Department of Travel and Immigration. I remember hearing about them creating this department. It's basically the friendlier version of the Department of Homeland Security. The powers that be thought it would sound nicer. I don't recall what their actual reason was, but that was the gist of it."

Heinrich sighs and says, "That's both encouraging and discouraging. We know that we'll be going back, but we don't know when. We also know that we have at least two more stops. I wish we were on that list. It'd be nice to see where we are going and when we will go back. Although, how would they know that part?"

"I am not sure how any of this works. It also looks like no one else knows either, but they are tracking it. The great thing so far is that you remember all of your stops and you can keep track for yourself how many there are. They did say a minimum of six jumps, so it could be more. I'm not trying to be a downer about it, but some of these had jumps into the double-digits. Think of it more as a heads up, that it could be quite the journey." Johann assures them.

Gustav smiles and nods, “I find that reassuring, and it means that we can enjoy our times for this one and the ones to follow. We are going to meet some great people, and hopefully we’ll continue to run into you guys and gals.”

“That would be great to see you along the way. The only thing is, we will age and you won’t.” Kat chuckles.

“The bonus is that Gustav and I are getting to see so many great things. I wonder what we will remember when we get back. It looks like some people remembered where they went enough to make a list. My question is, how does the government know this?”

Eddie speaks up, “The reason that the government knows is the travelers probably posted about it on their social media.”

“Social media, what’s that?” Heinrich inquires.

“It’s a place out on the internet where people communicate. It’s been around since the mid-1990s. For a while we weren’t sure if it would make it. Then there was a time that they got into censoring what was posted. Thankfully that didn’t last long. It’s so much easier for people to add things to social media. My favorite part is where it automatically uploads the pictures I take and I can speak the captions as I take them. Let’s look further into the information about these storms.” Johann pauses briefly, “It says that the storms are not necessarily predicted and can pop up at any time. That’s both encouraging and discouraging.”

AJ smiles, "You know, I think with that information, we need to go out and show these two the town. Let's maximize their time here. There's so much to see here. Why waste the time?"

They all nod, Johann shuts down his computer, and they get in the elevator. When they get to the first floor and the door opens there is a couple walking by. Heinrich and Gustav look at each other and simultaneously say, "William and Margaret!"

The couple turns around to see them getting out of the elevator. "Wait! Heinrich? Gustav? How is this possible? Did you guys come here right after our place?" William inquires.

Heinrich walks up to them and shakes their hands, "This is our second time jump since we saw you. Do you guys still live near the lighthouse?"

"Oh wow. Yes, Margaret and I still live near the lighthouse. We are over here on vacation. These festivals are so much fun that we had to come. So much has happened since we last you. However, we want to know, where did you jump to from our place?"

"We jumped to Rochester Castle where we met these great people. Thankfully when we jumped here it wasn't long and we met up with them again and now you two." Heinrich tells them and then introduces everyone.

Margaret asks, "Where are you all headed now?"

"We are going to show them around town. Do you want to join us?" Kat asks.

They both nod and say, “Yes, we’d love to.”

As they exit the hotel a few hot air balloons appear over the trees. Gustav exclaims, “Those are crazy designs! A seal, a lighthouse, and a bear. We have never seen anything like it!”

“Yes, this town always seems to have them nearby, but especially with this new Festival of Winter Balloons. There are so many special shapes including some specific for the Christmas and winter holiday season. We will be seeing more as we walk around town and then we’ll go over to the field to check out even more of them.” Johann explains.

The group walks over to the Holz Brücke and stops in the middle to look around. “I love this bridge and this scenery. The river is flowing in the center with the snow on the banks. The buildings we can see look Bavarian in style. Gustav and I are excited to see them close up.”

Continuing on, there are horses and buggies all decorated with lights. “Would everyone like to ride in a carriage for a tour of town?” Eddie asks.

Kat smiles and answers, “Of course, that’s the best way. Plus, they just added a bigger carriage so that we all can fit. I think it’s a nine passenger one. I know they have two horses pulling it.”

“I see it over by the restaurant. Let’s head over there. They will narrate the tour if we like, which is awesome because their drivers really know everything there is to know about this town." Johann tells them.

They are greeted as they walk up, "Welcome to Phantasiewagen. My name is Clint and I will be your driver. How many are in your party?"

"We have eight." Johann answers.

"Great. I can take you in this carriage with Niklas and Klaus guiding the way. Payment is made on your phones thru the Hier Bezahlen app."

Heinrich and Gustav look at each other confused. "What's an app?" Heinrich asks.

Johann tells them, "Don't worry about it. We've got this. I'll pay for the whole group."

"Great! There's a group discount." He tells them pointing at the pricing sign.

Everyone boards and pulls on their red blankets to help keep warmer. Once they are settled, the horses slowly start walking out of the parking lot.

Chapter 7

The snow fall transitions from light and fluffy to heavier and wetter. Clint explains, "Niklas and Klaus are strong Clydesdale horses. These guys can go through anything. During the ride, I will narrate some of the history of the town along with what's going on now. If you had ridden with us previously, you will notice that we now have speakers in the carriage. This makes it great because you can hear me and I don't have to yell."

Exiting out of the parking lot, they go through the covered bridge. "This is the Holz Brücke. They started building it 1977 and completed it in 1979 with a dedication in 1980. It contains 163,288 board feet of wood and nearly 1,000 pounds of non-wood material. It's one of our major attractions. Everyone wants their picture taken on or next to the Holz Brücke. Almost fifteen years ago they added a Riverwalk that starts just north of the bridge on the west side of the Cass River. From here, we will go through the parking lot of the Bavarian Inn Lodge."

Johann adds, "There's a nice Riverboat that you can go on during the non-winter months when the river isn't mainly frozen. Once in awhile you will see kayakers on the unfrozen portion of the path. They are the die-hards."

"You are correct Johann. Are you guys and gals staying at the Bavarian Inn Lodge?"

"Some of us are, yes." Kate pipes up.

“Great! This hotel has been in the Zehnder family since 1986. So, that makes it 49 years old. They also own the Bavarian Inn Restaurant. These two businesses are icons in the Frankenmuth area. To the right you can see the River Place Shops. That was added to the Zehnder’s portfolio in 2001 and hosts a lot of events and festivals including the new Winter Balloon Festival. The area that they let the balloons up will be coming up shortly on my right. We have quite a few special spaces to kick off this new festival.”

As they round the bend and the field comes into view, there are approximately a dozen balloons in various stages of inflation. “As you can see we have a nice variety of shapes. There’s an old-fashioned alarm clock, snowman, plus three different penguins in that far corner. It looks like the penguins are going up together. On the last day of the festival they are going to have a special Santa balloon. I can’t wait to see it.”

“When is the last day?” Margaret asks.

“That will be on Saturday the 8th. This is an unusual festival. We have most of the festival taking place through the week. It is amazing how many people come out during the week. Because of air temperatures the balloons go up in the evenings. We have received many messages from surrounding communities that the people are loving all the balloons going over or landing near them.”

Gustav questions, “Are they all in the different shapes?”

"Not all of them. Today is special shapes day because it's the first day of the festival. Tomorrow is the standard balloon shape, but all of them will be shades of red. Wednesday will be shades of green. Thursday will be blue and white for those that celebrate Hanukkah. Friday will be animal shapes. Finishing up on Saturday will be Christmas focused with the Santa balloon being the last one inflated."

"WOW! That is an awesome line-up. I am glad we are up here all week." AJ shouts.

Johann chuckles, "Seriously? You are loud. I do have to agree with you though, I am excited to see all of these balloons."

"This jump is the best one thus far. I can't wait to see what else there is and how do we top this one. Hopefully we can stay longer than we have with the others, which it has been getting a bit longer each time we jump." Heinrich says.

Gustav's eyes widen and questions loudly while pointing, "What is that?!"

"That is the vehicle dealership. It has a nice variety of all American made vehicles from motorcycles to cars to trucks. Plus it also has some that the locals use for around town, which are more in line with a golf cart."

"What's a golf cart?" Heinrich asks.

Eddie answers, "Oh yeah, these weren't invented until the 1930's. They are little carriages powered by a battery or gasoline. The golf cart orginally was invented to transport golfers around the golf course. Nowadays you see people doing all kinds of crazy things with them and never taking them to a golf course, but more likely riding around some small town during a festival."

Gustav and Heinrich both nod. Continuing along they ride past the Hero's Museum where there's a fighter jet out front. "That's cool. I am impressed that that is still around this many years later." Heinrich mentions.

"For this portion of our route we will be going to the end of this road, which will include Bronner's CHRISTmas Wonderland. This Christmas store is the largest in the United States and has been around since 1945. Currently, it sits at over 27 acres and the building is over 6 football fields in size. They are open 361 days a year and during this time of year it is absolutely crazy busy. I recommend coming in the off season during the week, and you'll be able to see all the decorations better. They have items from all over the globe. You could do multiple trees in multiple languages and cultures. In fact, they have displays just like that."

Kat mentions, "I love going there, but don't like the crowds, so I admire it from the outside as we get closer to Christmas. If you want a tour, hopefully you can come back during the summer."

"On the corner we have the Silent Night Chapel that was built in 1992. It's a replica of the St. Nicholas Chapel in Oberndorf, Austria. It's free to walk through, but does not do ceremonies. If you look to the left you will see the arch that says Auf

Wiedersehen on this side. It says Willkommen on the other side when you are driving into town."

As the go by Bronner's CHRISTmas Wonderland the interior road is lit up with all the Christmas decorations, most them made of lights, but a some are blown plastic. "In case you wanted to add to your own Christmas display with any of these decorations they are all available for sale. Even the Santa on the roof."

Heinrich says, "This is an amazing town. How much more is there? We've seen so much already."

Clint smiles and replies, "This is just the south end of town. We have a couple of miles to go to reach the north end and then head back to where we started. If you are amazed at what we've seen so far, you are in for a treat as we go into town. As we go by the houses, all are individually owned, and they have strict standards that they must maintain and follow.

Next up we have Rheingold's Splash Village Hotel and Indoor Waterpark. This is a great place to take kids or adults that want to act like kids. They have over 50,000 square feet of water fun. You can see the slides that come out of the building."

"We have stayed there with the boys and we all enjoyed it. My favorite part was the lazy river." AJ mentions.

Margaret asks, "How old are your boys?"

"They are twenty-one year old twins. Their names are Cooper and Carson."

"Nice, we too have boys. However, they are not twins. We have Donald and Dennis and they are in their fifties."

They continue through town with the garland and lights over the road and on all the houses along the way. "On our right here are the River Place Shops. This is a great outdoor shopping area with all kinds of specialty shops. I love the pedestrian bridge that leads to it with all the lights. It's like a tunnel of light. Below us is the Cass River. During the summer you will see people along the walkway and hear the riverboat. However, in the winter those are both closed. We do get some crazy kayakers that will traverse the river and rocks. The next traffic light brings us back by where we started. However, we will go on up the hill to get a great view of the entire town. You are not going to want to miss this."

The horses clip-clop along, as the roads are clear because they are all heated underneath. This enables the town to be able to clear the roads quicker. All the parking lots and sidewalks are designed the same way.

Clint continues, "There are many traffic lights in town and that is to keep the traffic speeds down and allow pedestrians to safely cross. Today is a slower day, as it's a Monday. The traffic will be triple this on the weekends, if not even more, depending on what festival is taking place. There are very few weekends that don't have a festival of some kind going on, especially in the summer. At the top of this hill is our brewery. It was destroyed by an F3 tornado in 1996. It took seven years before we got it back. Now, I highly recommend visiting it and having a few brews. Plus, they have great burgers."

They turn around at the end of town in the farmers' market parking lot. "On our way back, are there any places that you want to stop?" Clint asks.

"Hey, can we stop at Fritz's Fudge Shop? There's one thing you can't get enough of here and that is fudge. I love this stuff." Kat replies.

"As you wish. I do agree with you about the fudge. Does everyone have a favorite flavor?"

Kat offers, "dark chocolate fudge."

"I am a chocolate with peanut butter center," Eddie says.

AJ replies, "Johann and I like the rocky road."

"We are butter pecan fans," Margaret adds in.

Heinrich asks, "What's fudge?"

"It's a candy that is a combination of sugar, butter, and milk. Then flavors are added such as chocolate and nuts. It's cooked in a copper pot and cooled on a marble table. We make a few different shops that have it." Johann tells him.

"We are here, everyone can exit and I will wait for you. Enjoy!"

The group hops out of the carriage. “Welcome to Fritz’s! Come join us over here. We are paddling the fudge on the marble table. The current flavor that we are working on is the chocolate raspberry. My name is Fritz and my assistant is Lorenz.”

Heinrich and Gustav stand at the railing watching as they paddle it around and around. Margaret picks up salt water taffy and some fudge. Johann gets some dark chocolate peanut butter pucks to go with his fudge.

“I think we also should get some chocolate peanut butter toffee, too.” AJ says.

Kat tells her, “I had to have dark sea salt caramels to go with my dark chocolate fudge.”

“I am sensing a theme here.” AJ laughs.

The crew finishes their purchases and go back to the carriage. Everyone sits down and covers up with the red blankets.

“Alright, we are going back to where we started. I hope that you have enjoyed all the facts and history about our great town. Tell your friends about us and leave a review for us on social media. My name is Clint and the horses are Niklas and Klaus. Have a great evening.”

Walking away from the horses, the group crosses over the covered bridge back to their hotel. A few minutes later they are by the elevator. “Do you guys want to stay in our suite? We have plenty of room for two more." Johann asks Heinrich and Gustav.

They answer, "Yes."

Chapter 8

Heinrich opens his eyes and looks back and forth without moving his head. There are slivers of light coming in around the blinds. His mind starts racing, *Where am I? Am I still in Frankenmuth? It looks like the same room I went to sleep in.* Sitting up in bed, he glances over to the other bed and sees Gustav. He listens closely to see if he can hear any familiar voices.

"Good morning Heinrich, actually, is it morning? Are we still in Frankenmuth?"

"I don't hear anyone, yet. It looks like we are in the same room that we went to sleep in. I would guess, yes, we are still in the same place."

There's a knock at the door.

Heinrich and Gustav look at each other and then nod and smile.

"Who is it?" Heinrich asks.

"It's Johann. Is this Heinrich and Gustav?"

"Yes, we are here. What year is it?"

“It is still 2035. You guys have not time jumped, yet. Would you like to go to the breakfast buffet? We are all going there. It is in the hotel.”

Heinrich replies, “Yes, we will be out in a minute.” He turns to Gustav, “I am so glad to not have jumped yet, because I really like these people and this town. However, I’d love to get back to where we started. I really want to see cousin Karl.”

“I agree with you. What a rich history we learned last night. That Clint really knew his stuff. This festival looks like a lot of fun. The balloon styles and colors sound wonderful. My question is, how to remember all this stuff to take it all with us back to where we began?”

“That is an interesting idea that I hadn’t thought of. Maybe we write them down? We can ask Johann for pen and paper. Let’s go over there now.”

The travelers check themselves in the mirror and straighten their clothing and hair. When they open the door, they are greeted by Johann, AJ, Kat, and Eddie. “Hi guys!”

“We are glad that you guys are here still. The buffet is excellent. There are so many choices including potato pancakes, eggs, waffles, bratwurst, bacon, toast, and fruit.” Johann tells them.

Everyone goes down the elevator to Oma’s Restaurant. Greta is at the hostess station, “Welcome. How many?”

“We have six this morning.” Kat tells her.

“Follow me.”

They sit down to the round table. “We are only serving the breakfast buffet this morning. It is all you can eat and includes beverages. We have coffee, milk, and juice.”

“Coffee”

“Coffee”

“Chocolate milk for me” AJ smiles.

“Coffee”

“Coffee”

“Coffee”

“I will go get your beverages. You all can go up to the buffet.”

Greta walks off to the kitchen and the group goes up to the buffet. “Hey, these potato pancakes remind me of home. What’s this sauce here?” Heinrich asks.

AJ replies, “That is a hollandaise sauce. It’s made from egg yolk, melted butter, and lemon. This is goes on the sandwiches. It is one of my favs.”

The group makes their way along the buffet and back to the table and the coffees and hot chocolate are there.

Johann says, "I'm not sure how much longer you guys will be here, but I will enjoy our time, however brief. I did look further into information on time travel and it appears people are traveling and time hopping, like it's fairly common. I don't know how many others we've walked by that are time travelers, too. My research suggests that it's typically six time hops."

"I think it's great that they ended up in Frankenmuth because this is just like back home for them. What a perfect time for them to hop to and experience. 2035 is so much different from 1903. It's crazy how many years there are between the two." AJ adds in.

Heinrich replies, "Yes, it is very different. So much is different from what we are used to. Some of it has reminded me of home . When we first met you at Rochester Castle and now in Frankenmuth, I like it. I'm not sure what all this means. Does it mean we are going back home or does it mean that we are coming here? I don't know. I can't wait to see where we are going next. Will we be here in Michigan? Will we see you guys again? Will we see William and Margaret again?"

They continue to eat and drink their coffees and chocolate milk. People are coming in and filling up the tables.

Greta comes up to the table and asks, "Does anyone need anything else?"

They all shake their heads no.

"Your meals are included with your rooms. Have a great day and I hope to see you guys all again soon."

Everyone gets up from the table and exits to the outside of the Bavarian Inn Lodge. Standing out front, the group is watching the skies as it is filled with hot air balloons. Today is red balloon day.

Gustav looks at Heinrich and says, "This is breathtaking. Where do we go from here? Is this going to be the best place? Are we going to go further in time? Are we going back in time?"

Kat comments, "While you guys are here, let's enjoy our time together. However, can we figure out how to assist your jump time? Plus how can we help you predict where you are going to go to next and maybe even get you back to where you were?"

"How about we all go back up to the suite and look on the computer to see what has already been discovered as far as how they are time jumping?" Johann suggests.

The group turns around, and they go back up to the suite.

Opening his computer Johann discovers that the battery is dead and he forgot the plug. He turns to Eddie and shakes his head, while the group chuckles. AJ tells him, "I think I've got a plug in my bag. Let me go check." She disappears for a moment and returns with the cord in hand.

He takes the plug and gives her a big hug. "I don't know how it got into your bag, at least we have it we can move forward."

Plugging it in, it boots up immediately, and Johann's able to go right to the sites he has researched for time travel.

Meanwhile, outside the sky starts turning dark and the winds are picking up. The pilots are grounding the balloons and their crew securing them down. Everyone is moving swiftly.

Kat looks out the window, "Oh boy, it's getting dark outside and it's still morning. This is not good. Johann, how fast can you figure out how to predict where they are going next? It looks like it will be happening pretty soon."

"My computer only goes so fast. Granted, it is a pretty fast computer. So, hopefully we can get the information quickly." He's frantically typing on the keys.

The lights begin flickering. The group looks around at each other. There are flashes of lightning, and rumbles of thunder. All the lights come on, and then they go out. Johann grabs a flashlight from his computer bag next to his feet. He scans the room with it. Locating AJ, Kat, and then Eddie, he continues to look for Gustav and Heinrich. The lights flash back on. The group surveys the room and the travelers are nowhere in sight.

"We almost figured out where they were going." Eddie comments.

Smiling, AJ says, "I just hope that down the road we can see them again."

Chapter 9

The bright light diminishes and Heinrich opens eyes. Turning his head to the right he sees Gustav sitting next to him. He elbows him, "Hey, it's ok to open your eyes now. We have safely landed on a bench."

Blinking a few times, "Any idea where we are now?"

"Nope." Scanning around, "There's a nice brick gazebo over here and," leaning forward, "It looks like there's some buildings over there."

"Well, at least we landed safely." Gustav laughed.

"Yes we did. We'll have to go see where we are." They walk towards the road. It is busy with many trucks and vehicles. They wait patiently for the traffic signal to change. "I see there's a sign. It says "City of Wixom." We now know where we are. We are in the city of Wixom."

The travelers look both directions along the road and decide to walk towards the front of the two-story building near them. A train horn blows in the background and continues to get louder. As they walk, it comes into view ahead of them. "Wow is that moving fast. A lot of cars too." Heinrich comments.

As they are walking by the ice cream shop, the door opens. Anton and Pauline come out with another couple. Gustav says, “Fancy seeing you two here.”

They smile and shake hands. “Yes, let’s sit down over here.” Anton says and motions to the table. “Let me introduce everyone, Heinrich, Gustav, Cooper and Carla. We met Heinrich and Gustav on the Kroonland. Cooper and Carla here are helping us with our recent travels.”

“Glad to meet the two of you. I am guessing that your recent travels may be similar to ours. The great thing is that we have met some pretty good people along the way. In fact, we have even met up with some of them more than once. We hope that we will encounter them again. Where all have the two of you been?” Heinrich asks.

Anton smiles, “Yes, they are probably similar. It all started during that storm on the Kroonland. Is that where yours started?”

“That is when our travels started. I don’t know exactly where we were at, but our first time hop was onto another ship. It was the Edmund Fitzgerald, which we were told that it sank shortly after we got off of it.” Gustav explains.

“Pauline and I hopped first to a large waterfall named Niagara Falls. It was an awesome wonder. We met a couple by the names of Rudolfis and Karolina. They were also on the Kroonland. This means that we now have three sets of people from the Kroonland that are traveling through time. Where was your second time hop?”

Heinrich smiles, “We ended up in Ludington, Michigan near a lighthouse. This nice couple let us come in and shared their dinner with us. Their names were William and Margaret Robinson. What about you?”

The door opens to Pablo’s Mexican Restaurant and out walks Kat, AJ, Eddie, and the last one of the group was Johann. They walk towards the ice cream shop. Kat squeals with delight, “Heinrich! Gustav! You guys are here! I love it!” They stand up.

“Come meet our friends.” Heinrich tells them. “We have Anton and his wife Pauline. They were with us on the Kroonland. Our new friends Cooper and Carla are also friends of theirs.”

Johann laughs, “Yeah, we know Cooper and Carla very well. Cooper is one of AJ’s twin sons. Nice to meet you Anton and Pauline.”

“Wait! How do you guys know Heinrich and Gustav? You never mentioned them.” Cooper inquires.

AJ speaks up, “Actually, we did. You probably weren’t paying attention. You’d have been fifteen when they visited the castle. When we ran into them in Frankenmuth, you two were in honeymoon mode.”

“That makes sense. Well, now we are here. I can’t wait to hear all about all of the travels. Anton and Pauline went to different places.” Says Carla.

They all laugh. Another train horn blasts through town. Kat speaks loudly, "This is a great place to visit. Although, on certain days there is more train traffic than others. Right now they are delivering lots of packages between the local towns."

After a long line of cars, the train is off in the far distance, and it's easier to talk. Pauline speaks up, "I love all the Christmas decorations. This town is done up so well. It doesn't hold a candle to Frankenmuth. We ended up there on one of our time hops as well."

The group sits there and discusses what all they liked about Frankenmuth, which is a long list. There was nothing that they didn't like about it.

Fast-forward an hour, Eddie stands up, "This has been great to hear what all everyone likes about Frankenmuth. Now let's go to our place. We live right around the corner. It's not quite as nice as Johann's castle, but it's nice."

"Yeah, it may not be a castle, but it is a sprawling estate. Don't let him fool ya." Cooper scoffs.

Everyone walks around the building to the cars and goes over to Kat and Eddie's. They pull up to the black iron gate, which opens for their truck. Kat presses a button on an app that keeps it back for Johann and Cooper's vehicles. The gate closes behind the last one and the vehicles drive back to the house, which is about a half mile through the trees to a clearing.

They arrive in front of a two-story Cape Cod style mansion made of field stone and cedar. Eddie pulls into the six-car garage while the others park in the asphalt driveway. The group goes into the lower level entertainment room where there's a 12' diagonal touch screen computer on the wall. Kat presses on it, and it turns on with a couple dozen icons that are lit up.

Heinrich looks at it, "That is huge! Every time we meet with you guys, these things get bigger and bigger."

"Yeah, I had to have this one. I love being able to multitask to bring up smaller screens all at the same time. The best part is that I can click on one of the icons, and it pulls up all the screens that are saved to it. This one here is linked to a group that Johann and I have been sharing about the time travels. So, let's take a look at it." Eddie smirks.

As he touches the old notebook shaped icon, a dozen screens appear on the wall each with a different website on it. Johann walks up to the screens, "We have been able to find hundreds of people that have also traveled through time. As we had mentioned in Frankenmuth ten years ago, they are each having at least six time hops per time travel journey. They have also found that some people go more than once. So, just because you get back to your starting point doesn't mean that your time travel journeys are necessarily over."

"Have you figured out how to predict it? You know, like how do we start it? Can we pick where and when we go to?" Heinrich asks.

Eddie answers, "At this point, we have only been able to track after the fact, where everyone went. The one thing they all have in common is when there's a storm, even if the weather doesn't look a storm is coming. I mean, look at Frankenmuth, when we were there, there was no warning of a storm. The balloons were going up and if they knew there was going to be a storm, they would not go up in the first place."

"The great part is that every time someone time hops, we are able to record it." pointing to the screen. "This site is where there is a bunch of contributors that add to it when they have a time traveler visit. We record who it is, include any time hop information that is not already in the database, and add the new visit as well." Johann tells them.

Kat stands up again, "I want to make sure that everyone knows that we have plenty of rooms for all to stay the night. No worries about driving home or finding some place to sleep. I mean, we do have six bedrooms plus a guest house with two more. Who wants a tour?"

"Maybe we can do that after we get done here, honey." He smiles at her and continues, "Although, if you gals want to go upstairs and bring down some of those awesome Christmas treats that you've been making. We could go for some."

She rolls her eyes at him, smiles, and motions for AJ and Carla to follow her. The three take the elevator up to the main kitchen.

The sun is starting to set and all the Christmas lights turn on, inside and out. There is a trio of trees in the corner of the entertainment room near the screens. Each is decorated in a different color, purple, red, and green. Heinrich admires them, "I understand the red and the green colors for decorations. However, what's up with the purple?"

"Purple is Kat's favorite color. I think it's also AJ's. When they decorate the trees here and at the castle, at least one purple one is included." Eddie explains.

Heinrich smiles, "Yes, a women's preference, that makes sense."

A few moments later the ladies return with a few trays of Christmas treats. They place them on the buffet and take a seat on the couches.

The guys continue updating the database with the time hops of Heinrich and Gustav. A bit of time goes by and Kat pipes up, "Hey, do you guys want the goodies that we brought down?"

"Ok, we'll take a break for the evening." Johann replies with a smile. The group gathers at the buffet and enjoys the treats.

Chapter 10

The next morning the smell of eggs and bacon wafting through the home lures Eddie into the kitchen where Kat is cooking. Minute by minute Cooper, Carla, Heinrich, Gustav, Johann, AJ, Pauline, and Anton enter the kitchen.

“Breakfast is ready. Everyone can have a seat at the dining room table. We have bacon, eggs, fruit, and toast. I hope that you all enjoy it.” Kat tells them. AJ helps her set everything on the table, and the rest of the crew sits down.

While at the table Johann speaks up, “Please continue enjoying your meal. I want to go over a few things. One, is I am happy to see everyone this morning. Two, this breakfast is awesome–Thanks Kat. Third, we are going to have a great day figuring out this time travel. I cannot wait to hear all about the travels of Anton and Pauline.”

“We have been on quite the journey. Each time hop brought us closer and closer to this location. How about you guys?” Anton asks.

Gustav takes his last bite, “This is a wonderful breakfast. Thank you, Kat. For our travels, it’s been primarily here in Michigan. I’m not sure on the first time hop. We were on the Edmund Fitzgerald in open water and not near land.”

"You were in Michigan then too. The Edmund Fitzgerald sank shortly after you guys got off of it, in Lake Superior, which is between Michigan and Canada. It sank in the Michigan waters. I can show you when we go in the other room." Cooper informs them.

He smiles and his eyes widen, "I am glad we got off the ship at the right time. That also means all of our time hops were in Michigan. Anton had mentioned one of your time hops was in New York. Where were the rest of them?"

"We'll go over all that in the other room when everyone is done with breakfast." Johann tells them.

A few minutes later the group gets up one by one, puts their dishes in the sink, and heads for the computer area. Eddie touches the screen and it turns on again. "Ok, Anton, let's map out your time hops. The first one you said was Niagara Falls. Do you remember what year that you landed in?"

He walks up to Eddie and says, "We hopped to December 1975. It was so beautiful. The water flowed, but there was snow and ice around it. We were only there for a few hours. Then we hopped to December 2001, and we were in the town of Marblehead, Ohio by a lighthouse. The next time hop was to December, 2028. We hopped into Frankenmuth, Michigan and loved it."

Eddie placed markers on the map on one screen while on another he entered the time hop information into the database. Kat brought over glasses of water for everyone.

"These are all great places. I think the consensus is that everyone loves Frankenmuth and it doesn't matter when they land there." Johann says.

Anton continues, "Yes, we loved the horses and the small Bavarian town charm. It'd be great to go there again. Our next time hop was then to December, 2035 and we ended up in Marquette, Michigan. That was super cold and quite a few feet of snow. The large log cabin mansion was beautiful. It was right on Lake Superior. We could see far out into the distance and it hadn't completely frozen over."

The last few data pieces are entered and Eddie announces, "All the time hops are in!" He pauses for a moment, "I find it interesting that the time hop years were the same. However, there was only one duplicate city and it was Frankenmuth. It is the most Christmassy town there is, no matter the year."

One of the screens appears with the camera on the front gate. It shows Vicki with Carl and Anna pulling in and driving up to the house. A few minutes pass, and they come into the entertainment area. "Hi!" Everyone shouts.

"Well, who are these two? I recognize the rest of you." Carl inquires.

"I am Anton and this is Pauline. We are also time travelers. We started out with Heinrich and Gustav on the Kroonland. Just before you got here we were sharing our time hops."

The three sit down and join them. Kat brings over more glasses of water. Eddie touches an icon on the screen and it brings up a map of all the Christmas lights on their property–both inside and out. “I think that we need the Christmas lights on early today. They always add extra cheer.”

There’s another icon that he presses and a music player comes up containing Christmas play list. “I love this list. It has a huge variety of genres and it has thousands of songs on it.” Kat tells them.

The music plays, they get up, and dance around the room. This goes on for an hour when there’s a screen that appears with a request for a video call from Axel Krauss–the original. Eddie touches the “Answer” button. “Hey! What’s up?”

“I was wondering if you had any more encounters with time travelers.”

“Yes, in fact, we have four of them here. Heinrich, Gustav, Anton, and Pauline. They are all from the Kroonland. What about you?”

“Lizzie and I have Ludwig and Julia here. They were on the Kroonland too. What in the world happened on that ship? We have three pairs that were on it. It’s just crazy!”

“Have you updated the time hop database?” Axel inquires.

“I have entered their travels into the computer.” Eddie responds.

“I heard about the tree lighting and Christmas festival in the park today. Are you going?”

Kat chimes in, “We are all going. Wouldn’t miss it. We will have the group all together. Then afterwards, we’ll come back to our place for some more celebrating. There will be treats and a hot cocoa bar.”

“I love your hot cocoa bars. You do such a great job of them.” Lizzie says with a beaming smile.

“We’ll see everyone there.” Eddie says and he closes the screen. Turning to the group he asks, “What do we want to do until we leave for the festival? I know! How about we go for a helicopter ride? We just got a brand new Hubschrauber 95XI. It will hold all of us.”

The group goes out to the hanger that is behind the outdoor spa area. Eddie pulls it out using a helicopter-dolly. Once out on the pad, he opens the door for all to board. Anton, Pauline, Heinrich, and Gustav stand there staring at the large helicopter.

“ What is this?” Heinrich questions.

Eddie smiles, “It’s my new favorite mode of transportation. Also known as a helicopter. They were invented in 1907, so after you arrive in America. I know you probably have only heard of Wilbur and Orville playing with airplanes. This is similar to an airplane, being that it takes off straight up instead of needing a runway. It makes it easier to have at home, because it takes up less space. For planes, the propellers will be on the front, whereas these are up top. We have headsets for everyone to wear on their ears and talk into the microphone."

The four board the helicopter and sit down. Eddie is careful to seat everyone appropriately to insure balance and stability during their flight. Kat assists them with their seatbelts and headsets. A few minutes later, Eddie is taking off and flying over the city and countryside.

"I hope everyone will enjoy their ride. We are going over Wixom and will be flying over downtown Rochester within a few minutes or so. You are going to love all the lights. The entire town is covered in them."

He leans the helicopter to one side, enabling them to see the buildings all lit up better. When he reaches the edge of town, he turns around and leans the other way for everyone else to see.

Upon reaching the other end of town, Eddie flies over Rochester Castle, "Check out Johann and AJ's Christmas decorations. They went all out this year."

"Yes, we did. Burchard got us even more lights. I didn't think it was possible." Johann tells them.

They fly back to the helicopter pad and land. "Thank you for this. It is certainly a once in a lifetime thing to do." Heinrich says.

The group exits the helicopter and gets in the vehicles to go into Wixom for the Christmas tree lighting and festival.

Chapter 11

The snow is blowing as the group parks across from the festival. There are dozens of short trees with lights and decorations. In the middle of the park is a twenty-foot tree that is filled with handmade decorations.

People continue to gather around the Christmas tree. A ten-piece band is playing on the stage next it. The Mayor takes the microphone, "Welcome everyone to the Wixom Christmas Festival! This year we have two dozen trees around this city area along with this large one that are becautifully decorated by children of all ages from all of our schools and day-cares. Our countdown to the tree lighting will begin in ten minutes. Grab your hot cocoas and candy canes. Don't forget to get your large bulb necklaces from our marching band students."

Axel and Lizzie along with Ludwig and Julia walk up to the group, "Hi!"

"Isn't this great? We have six time travelers here! I hear they know of a couple more from the same ship." Lizzie says.

Kat gives Lizzie a hug, "Yes, it is so wonderful. The four at our place have hopped to the same years, but for the most part different locations. They did have Frankenmuth in common."

"So, that is eight people from the same ship that have time traveled. We'll have to compare notes to see if they all went to the same time hops."

"Yes we will. We can do it when we are back at our place for the hot cocoa bar."

Axel leans over Lizzie, "I am all for the hot cocoa bar. You usually have great treats to go with them too."

Johann motions everyone to gather close together and takes some photos of the group, along with the decorations and trees.

A semi horn blows, the band begins to play "Here Comes Santa Claus," and a large red truck comes into view that is covered in lights. It pulls down and around to have the lowboy trailer next to the park with Santa's sleigh and reindeer.

"Welcome Santa! We are happy to have you here with this for our tree lighting. Only a few more days until the big night. Come on up to the mic and say a few words." The Mayor hands the mic over to him.

Santa shakes some bells and says, "Thank you city of Wixom! I see a lot of good boys and girls are here. You are all on my nice list. The reindeer are resting up for the big night and love the ride on the back of the semi."

"Are you ready for Santa to light the tree?"

The crowd yells, "YES!"

Santa grabs the light controller arm, “Count down with me!”

“10, 9, 8, 7, 6, 5, 4, 3, 2, 1!” He pulls the arm and all the lights go on.

The crowd erupts in cheers.

Eddie asks their group, “Now the tree is lit, how about we go back to our place and we have our own celebration?”

Everyone nods and they walk back to their vehicles. Within a few minutes, they are driving through the trees to the mansion. Upon arrival the group gathers on the entertainment deck. The backyard is lit up and the Christmas music is playing over the outdoor speakers.

Kat asks the ladies, “Can I get some help bringing out the hot cocoa bar and treats?” AJ, Carla, and Lizzie follow her into the kitchen. Within minutes they reappear with multiple carts of goodies.

“Everything is ready. Help yourselves to the hot cocoa and all the treats. There’s plenty.” She announces.

The evening rolls on and Axel asks, “Hey, how about we compare notes on who traveled when and where?”

“Sounds like a good idea. I have everything in the entertainment room inside. Let’s bring all the stuff in and we’ll go over it.” Eddie replies.

Pushing the carts inside, the ladies reset the treats. Eddie brings up the database with the time hops. “Ok, let’s go over the travels. I will list Heinrich and Gustav first and then Anton and Pauline. The first hop was to 1975 and they went to the Edmund Fitzgerald and Niagara Falls. The second hop was to 2001 where one went to Ludington, Michigan and the other to Marblehead, Ohio. The third one was in 2028 where we met them in Rochester, Michigan. The others went to Frankenmuth. Then the fourth time hop was in 2035 to Frankenmuth and Marquette. Finally here to 2045 near Wixom. Where did Ludwig and Julia go to?”

“They had the same years, but different locations. They went to Frankenmuth in 1975, Traverse City in 2001, St. Joseph in 2028, and Port Huron in 2035. A lot of traveling and also interesting that they didn’t end up in the same spots until now. I wonder what is next?” Axel questions.

Eddie plots all of the locations on a map. “It’s incredible how much of their time is spent in Michigan. The majority of the stops are in the mitten. Only two of them were not.”

“We are getting so close to Christmas. I hope you guys and gals are all here for a few more days. What a great way for us to all celebrate the holiday.” Lizzie says.

The fire in the hearth spreads warmth through the room. Everyone gathers closer with their mugs of hot cocoa and plates of treats. They sing Christmas songs for the next hour.

As they sit there, they can hear the roar of the trees blowing in the wind. It keeps getting louder and louder. "Good thing we have a good generator." Eddie chuckles.

Streaks of lightning light up the skies and the thunder cracks so hard that the ground shakes. Everything goes dark for a few minutes. When the generator kicks on, the group looks around to see who all is still there. The time travelers are all gone.

"I'm bummed to see them all gone, but where will they end up?" Carla asks.

Cooper answers, "That's a good question. Hopefully we will see them again."

Chapter 12

Black clouds blanket the area, lightning streaks through the sky. Heinrich looks around and finds Gustav sitting in a chair next to him. As he scans across the patio he discovers Anton, Pauline, Rudolfis, Karolina, Ludwig, and Julia.

“Ok, everyone, where do you think we are?” Heinrich asks.

Gustav smiles, “I know. I am really pleased to say that we are at the Rochester Castle. I recognize the facade. The real question is, what day is it?”

“I take it, you two have been here and it’s friendly to travelers.” Anton says.

“Yes, Gustav and I have been here previously. This is where Johann and AJ live.” Heinrich stands up and knocks on the door.

Burchard opens the door, “Welcome!” He turns to the people inside, “Gang! Heinrich and friends are here.” Turning back to outside, “Come on in everyone! Welcome! Welcome!”

The group gets up and goes inside. Burchard shows them to the living room where the friends are sitting. They stand up and shake hands.

Johann says, “I am glad to see you all here. We never knew when or if you’d be back. I see we have all four pairs. The question that you all are asking yourselves is, what is today’s date? I know you are, because I would be asking it. It is Christmas Eve 2050. This is also why we are all here. Thankfully we decided to celebrate at the castle instead of out at the mansion or the farm. Our ladies have prepared a great feast. The good thing is, they always make food for an army, and we normally have leftovers for days. So, we have plenty for everyone. The table is currently set for fourteen. We can set eight more spots. I am glad we have a large dining hall that was added on.” He motions for everyone to go to the dining hall.

“Welcome to our Christmas Eve dinner. Carson and Cooper, I need some assistance to add more place settings.” AJ requests.

The guys bring out more plates, silverware, and glasses. The gals carry out the trays of food, and they all sit down around the filled table.

Over the next twenty minutes the table is void of conversation as the friends are enjoying their meal. Heinrich speaks up, “This has been a great welcome. It feels like we are home. Although, we know that we are going back to our own time in history at some point, We will enjoy our time here while we can.”

“We know all about everyone, except for Rudolfis and Karolina. Where all have you two been?” Johann asks.

Setting down his fork, Rudolfis answers, “Our first time hop we ran into Anton and Pauline in Niagara Falls. That was a great stop. I love waterfalls and this one was large. Has everyone been?”

Everyone nods, except for Anna. “I haven’t been, yet. Carl and I plan on going there this spring.”

“You will want to make sure and go behind the falls. Karolina loved it. Our next hop was into Frankenmuth in December 2001. That town really knows how to celebrate Christmas. From there we went to Marquette and that was in December 2028. The snow fall there was unbelievable.”

Anton injects, “We were there in December 2035, and it was beautiful, but I agree with the amount of snow fall.”

“We then hopped to St. Joseph in December 2035. The lighthouse was covered in ice and the winds were crazy. After that St. Joseph we went to Ludington in December 2045. While we were there William and Margaret told us all about all of you. I was pleasantly surprised when we hopped here with everyone. This is great! Do we know what this means? Does it mean we are all going back to the ship?” Rudolfis questions.

Johann answers, “We don’t know yet, but this is time hop number six and that is normally how many there are before returning. Hopefully that’s a good thing. I do love all the locations that everyone has been to. After dessert, we are going into the living room where we’ll be doing a story. You’ll like it. We will enjoy as much time as we have together.”

AJ disappears into the kitchen and returns pushing a cart with three large trays of desserts. “Well gang, we have a nice variety of treats. We have prepared for you chocolate chip cookie dough fudge, mini cannolis, corn flake wreaths, mini apple tarts, snow angel cookies, Spritzgebäck, pfeffernuesse cookies, Vanillekipferl, Zimtsterne, Kaiser-Plätzchen, mini soft pretzels, and stollen bread. I hope that everyone will enjoy!”

“These look wonderful! You made all these German treats, but how did you know that we’d be here?” Pauline asks.

Assisting with placing the trays on the table, Anna answers, “She’s been researching German cooking and we’ve been her guinea pigs and helpers. It’s been great. We always hope that you will return each year. The ones that you weren’t here for, we gave a toast to each of you.”

Everyone fills their plates with yummy treats. The Christmas music softly plays in the background. Snow is falling outside the windows.

“I know the German treats, but some of these I don’t recognize.” Gustav inquires while still chewing on a corn flake wreath.

Chuckling, Cooper replies, “Well, what you are eating is a corn flake wreath. It’s a very popular Christmas treat here in the US. It’s made with a corn flake cereal, melted marshmallows, and cinnamon red-hot candies. One of my many favs that mom makes.”

“My personal fav is the chocolate chip cookie dough fudge.” Carson adds in.

Holding up a mini cannoli with mini chocolate chips on the ends, “This is my new fav. AJ started making them a few years back after finding the recipe on social media.” Johann tells them.

“I have a non-food question. How is everyone related or are you all friends?” Ludwig asks.

Standing up, Cooper explains, “Let me clarify it for you. Johann, the owner of this awesome castle, is married to my mom, AJ. Carla is my wife. Carson is my twin brother with his wife, Laila. Kat is Johann’s sister and married to Eddie Laufer. Carl is Johann’s brother and married to Anna. Lizzie is Eddie’s sister and married to Axel. Vicki is best friends with AJ and Kat plus married to Otis.”

“I didn’t realize that Johann and AJ were married when we first met them here.” Heinrich comments.

With a large smile on her face, AJ replies, “We weren’t married when we met you guys back in 2028. We tied the knot in 2031.”

“You guys are almost to your twentieth anniversary.” Julia remarks.

Johann gets up from the table, “How about we all go into the living room? We can sit around the Christmas tree, and before you ask, yes, we can take the treats in there. Bring your beverage as well.”

“We have a game that we play and it'll be a lot of fun.” Vicki adds.

Carl says, “This was my brother's idea, and it gets better every year. I highly recommend it.”

The group grabs the plates of goodies along with their drinks and goes to the living room.

Chapter 13

The tree is lit and the garland is all around the ceiling and across the fireplace hearth. AJ takes a seat by the crackling fire and picks up a book. "For our new friends, let me share with you a tradition that we have. I have a book here that has a bunch of story starters. I will read the story starter and then we go around the room and each person adds a bit to it. We record the session and afterwards, Kat will transcribe it into a book format. We then have it for future generations."

Karolina says, "What a great idea. Do you want us to participate this year?"

"Most certainly we do. This will make it even more special." Kat answers for AJ.

Eddie adds, "I think it will be great to have all of you in our story this year."

"I agree with them. Let me start off with this year's story starter, and we'll go around the room and have you guys join in after you see what we do. Are you ready to record Kat?"

"Yes, please begin."

"It's the night before Christmas and Sugar Firewine, the Christmas elf, is sitting at her desk staring at a piece of paper." AJ starts.

Johann continues, "Tinsel Sparklefeast tiptoes up behind her and taps her on the shoulder. Sugar jumps, hitting her knees on the bottom of the desk. "Ouch! Don't do that! You scared me!" She yelled."

"Tinsel laughs and runs away. Sugar rolls her eyes and goes back to staring at her paper." Cooper adds.

Carla says, "Fairy dust erupts from the paper. Two unicorns fly out and circle around the room."

"Dasher and Dancer fly in from the barn and chase after the unicorns." Carson joins in.

Laila laughs and continues the story, "The four leave the room and head out to the yard. Shortly all the reindeer are flying around chasing the unicorns."

Everyone is laughing, eating treats, and drinking their beverages.

"Santa runs out shouting, "Dasher, Dancer, Prancer, Vixon, Comet, Cupid, Donner, and Blitzen, into the barn!"" Carl performs.

Taking a drink of her hot cocoa, clearing her throat, Anna says, "The reindeer continue to ignore Santa. Mrs. Claus comes out of the house with freshly made carrot cookies. They all turn and stop right in front of her."

"Tinsel runs out from the house with her paper, waving it in the air towards the unicorns. She lays it on the ground, and they fly right into the fairy dust bursting out of the paper." Lizzie tells.

Axel stands up and pronounces, "More elves come running from the shop. The snow falls faster and faster. The northern lights get brighter, and the Christmas music gets louder."

"Santa's sleigh sits in the barn. The elves come in and start throwing packages into a big red bag. A few minutes later the reindeer all line up in their spots." Otis moves the scene.

Vicki smiles, "Santa and Mrs Claus enter the barn. "Safe travels and enjoy those cookies." She tells him. He hops into the sleigh and picks up the reigns. The elves throw the bag into the back. Santa snaps the reigns and yells, "Let's go boys!""

"The reindeer take off, flying out of the barn, and speed off into the night. They head for their first stop, which is Christmas Island." Kat proudly says.

Eddie sits up straight after putting his cookie down, "As they get closer, all the lights are out on the island. The reindeer turn on their noses to help see the way."

"Ok, we have all added to the story. Do you eight want to join in?" Johann inquires.

They all nod their heads and smile. Pointing at one another to start.

“I’ll give this a go.” Rudolfis comes forward, “Santa lands the sleigh on a rooftop, wrinkles his nose, and appears in the house with the presents to put under the tree.”

Karolina joins in, “The family cat growls at him, as it is hidden under the tree. Santa lays down some cat treats, and it comes out. The cat sits there purring. Within moments, Santa disappears from the house and returns to the sleigh.”

“He finds some military personnel marching down the street. The stop in their tracks as they view the sleigh and reindeer.” Gustav adds.

Heinrich takes a turn, “Santa moves the sleigh and reindeer down to the military personnel, and hands out small presents for them all. As he leaves them, they try not to smile.”

“Within minutes he has delivered all the packages to the island and flies to the next one.” Pauline chimes in.

Anton thinks for a few seconds, “The time passes by quickly, and he makes his way to all the homes. He gets to the last house in America.”

“Where he is met by the family dog. It does not make a good guard dog, but goes up to Santa and licks him while wagging his tail.” Julia smiles.

Ludwig puts down his beverage, "After petting the dog, Santa finishes placing the presents and goes back to his sleigh. With the wink of an eye, he flashes to the North Pole where Mrs. Claus is waiting for him."

Kat turns off the recording. "This will be a fabulous addition to our book of stories."

The group sits while the fire crackles and the lights twinkle. Johann turns up the Christmas music. Time goes by, and soon it is a few hours later.

"Ok, it's late and Christmas is quickly approaching. We do have rooms for everyone. Tomorrow's breakfast is going to be fabulous. I can't wait for you all to enjoy it. Come follow us and we will show you to your room." AJ tells them.

Turning off the music and lights, Johann guides them through the castle to where each will be staying.

Chapter 14

The castle is quiet, the darkness is broken by slivers of light peeking through the blinds. Christmas music starts playing throughout. The lights automatically come on, thanks to the timer that Johann had previously set.

Carson and Cooper sneak into the living room. They fill all the stockings and add some for the time travelers. Quiet as church mice, they go back to their rooms.

Moments later, AJ and Johann slide down to the kitchen. "I hope they enjoy this breakfast. I'll get making the French toast with the cinnamon rolls. Can you work on the bacon? The smell of that will definitely get everyone down here."

"Yes, I love the bacon. We have a few packages of it. I will put it on trays in the oven. Should I add some maple syrup and brown sugar to it or leave it as is?"

"Leave it as is. I got the applewood smoked bacon. It has great flavor. Plus, the cinnamon rolls are going to be sweet. We don't want to over power them with sweets this early. We have all day." She laughs.

"Good idea. We still have so many sweet treats for them to snack on all day."

Vicki walks into the kitchen, “Merry Christmas! Do you need any help?”

“Can you get the table for us? There’s what eight plus fourteen. So, we are looking at twenty-two. We have enough for twenty-four. Set them all out, you never know if we have a drop-in visitor or two.” AJ states.

Vicki goes to the pantry where the dishes are and places them on a cart. She is the perfect person to have set the table, as she is the one that knows where all the pieces go properly.

A few minutes later, Otis appears in the dining area and helps Vicki with the place settings. She gives the instructions on where everything goes.

Carson, Carla, Cooper, and Laila enter the kitchen. “What do you need from us?” Cooper asks as he gives his mom a kiss on the cheek.

“It would be great if you all could help with slicing up the cinnamon rolls. I am making the egg mixture for the French toast. I will then need the guys to help with getting all these dipped and put on the griddles.”

Kat and Eddie peek around the corner into the kitchen, “Merry Christmas!”

“Merry Christmas!” Everyone replies.

"We will be in the living room setting up for the festivities or are we going to use the entertainment room in the basement?" Eddie questions.

Johann looks up from his tray of bacon, "Let's go into the entertainment room. We have a couple of trees in there. We'll do stockings in the living room and then move downstairs."

They disappear to the basement to bring out all of the red and green decorations. "I am also using purple. AJ loves that color." Kat tells him.

Lizzie and Axel walk into the dining room, "Merry Christmas. Do you need any help?"

"Yes, please. I have one place setting complete and it's going to be for twenty-four people. So, if you can help, that'd be great." She answers them.

AJ looks at Johann, "I haven't seen your brother and sister-in-law yet. You might want to go check on them."

"Yes, I will be back in a few." He leaves the kitchen and bounds upstairs to Carl and Anna's room. Knocking on the door, "Hey, you guys in there?"

Anna replies, "We are in here. Be down in a few."

Johann returns back to the kitchen, "They'll be here in a bit."

In the meantime, the travelers all appear in the kitchen. AJ says to them, "Frohe Weihnachten!"

"Frohe Weihnachten!" They all reply.

"Welcome to Christmas morning. We are making breakfast and the table should be all set. After we eat, everyone will go to the living room to open our stockings." Johann lets them know.

The group goes to the dining room and choose which chairs they will sit in. A few minutes later, they are joined by Carl and Anna.

"Hi everyone! Merry Christmas! So glad to see all of you." Carl says.

Heinrich replies, "It's always interesting when we wake up to see where we are. I am happy to see that we are still here. This has been quite the trip. My biggest question is, will we remember all of this when we go back to where we started?"

The kitchen crew comes in with carts of food and places the trays on the table. "Are we ready to eat?" AJ inquires.

"Yes!" everybody responds.

AJ smiles, "In front of you is French toast that is made with cinnamon rolls. Plus there is bacon. We also have fresh fruit. Dig in and enjoy!"

"Before we start to eat. I want to say that I am very thankful that we have a full table with extra guests this year. We did not know if you would be joining us or not. Each year we hoped to hear from you and this time we got our wish. Thank you for joining us." Johann tells them.

Anton raises his glass, "I want to give a toast to all of our new friends. You guys and gals have taken it in stride, every time you have hosted some or all of us time travelers. This has been crazy. I am mixed about going back to my original time. I have enjoyed the new things and all of you. What we don't know is if we will remember all of you when we go back. In case we don't, I truly appreciate all of you." All glasses rise up in unison.

They grab French toast and bacon, placing it on their plates. For several minutes the only sounds you hear are of contented diners. Finally, it changes to silverware being laid down on empty plates and sighs of being full

"I know that I am one of the youngest ones here, even if I am not a little kid. I am still a kid at heart. Are we ready to go to the living room for stockings?" Carson questions.

AJ laughs, "Yes, if everyone is finished, we can go into the living room. We will leave the dishes here for the time being. Are we all ready to open our Christmas stockings?"

Looking back and forth to each other, they all smile and nod yes.

"Ok then, let's go into the living room." She says.

The friends push out their chairs and move to the next room, leaving the table full of dishes and glasses. Walking by the tin soldier in the entryway, they all grab a hand-made candy cane from the basket it was holding, and continue on their way to the living room.

Gathering around the Christmas tree that is set proudly to the right of the fireplace. Everyone takes a seat, except for Johann. He is standing next to the hearth.

"I want to wish all of you a very Merry Christmas and Frohe Weihnachten! We traditionally gather in this room to enjoy the fireplace and conversation. There's no television in here for that exact reason. We want to talk with one another. Today is a joyous Christmas Day or Weihnachten for our guests. What a pleasure it is every time we have you here, whether it's just a couple of you or all of you. Each year we gather, we pass out stockings with little gifts. This time the mantle is more full, as every one of you have one with your name on it. My helper, Carson, is going to hand them out. Please wait to open them until everyone has theirs."

He joins him at the hearth, reading the names out loud as he hands them to the person, "AJ, Johann, Cooper, Carla, myself, Laila, Carl, Anna, Eddie, Kat, Axel, Lizzie, Otis, Vicki, Heinrich, Gustav, Anton, Pauline, Ludwig, Julia, Rudolfis, and Karolina. We can open them now."

Some dump the stocking contents on their laps, others carefully take out each item, and then there are those that gently slide the stuff out onto their laps.

"Everyone's stockings are filled with treats. We want to be careful that when our travelers go back to their time that they don't take anything from the future. That could be very confusing for those around them. I hope that it's enjoyable. Next up we will go to the entertainment room. We will walk through the pub to find the entertainment room. I believe Heinrich and Gustav were down there when they first arrived." Johann shares.

They smile and Heinrich says, "Yes we were and we were impressed by getting German beer."

"That we do have and lots of it. Since you were here, we did add on to the castle. The five bedrooms were perfect for a while, but we needed more for visitors. Each new one has a walk-in closet and a hot tub. We also converted the underground garage to our entertainment room. It's easily entered by guests that are here only for an evening while also being close to our pub. The lighted ceiling was expanded and a sound system installed throughout the castle including in the entertainment room. Oh yes, we have added solar power and a natural gas generator, which has really helped us with cutting costs and always having power."

Johann and Carson motioned for them to follow along as they leave the room to go downstairs and through the pub to the new entertainment area.

The room is dark with the ceiling lights twinkling like stars. A purple and gold tree highlights a far corner. As Johann enters, the Christmas music begins to play. He turns up the wall sconces to half power with the alternating green and red colors.

Johann motions for AJ's hand to dance. She accepts, and they twirl around the dark brown hickory hardwood floor. Within minutes the other couples join them. Johann bows out and lets Heinrich dance with AJ. Eddie follows suit and pairs Gustav with Kat. As the music and time continues, all the dancers are switched back and forth and all around.

He commands, "Music down please." After a pause, "I hope that everyone is enjoying themselves. This Christmas dance is going to continue with access to the pub area. Very soon we will be joined by other friends."

Within moments there's a knock on the door. Carl answers it, "Welcome to the Rochester Castle Christmas Dance. Please come in. There are beverages and treats in the pub area."

People continue to arrive throughout the afternoon. Some stay long enough to offer their message of Merry Christmas to everyone, while others are there for hours. The pub area is busy with dancers taking a snack and beverage break.

Johann announces, "I want to recognize these wonderful ladies. Kat, Vicki, and AJ have put together an assortment of treats for us.

Kat worked on the no bake items of rum balls, corn flake wreaths, buckeyes, chocolate covered pretzels, chocolate chip cookie dough fudge, and hard rock candy.

Vicki contributed with the mini apple tarts, snow angel cookies, Spritzgebäck, sugar cookies, pizzelles, and mini cannolis.

AJ made the pfeffernuesse cookies, Vanillekipferl, Zimtsterne, Kaiser-Plätzchen, mini soft pretzels, and stollen bread. We hope that everyone will enjoy them."

"What he hasn't told you is about the large assortment of beers he has from around the globe. That list is too long to go through and we'd probably miss something anyways. You'll have to go check that out for yourself. For those that don't do beer, he has a complete wine cellar along with some non-alcoholic beverages. There's something for everyone." Carl informs them.

The day continues with eating, drinking, and dancing to Christmas music. There's another knock at the door, but it's different from others, this has a jingle with it. Everyone stops what they are doing and looks on as Johann opens it.

"Welcome! Willkommen!" He motions for the person to enter.

In walks a white bearded man in a red hat and suit with black boots.

"Merry Christmas! Frohe Weihnachten!" He proclaims as he crosses the room to the chair next to the tree.

Laying down his black sack and sitting he says, "Who has been good this year?"

The group gathers around him, while he passes out gifts. His sack empties within minutes and everyone disperses throughout the room.

Standing up, Santa makes his way to the door. Turning around to the crowd he says, “Frohe Weihnachten an alle und allen eine gute Nacht.”

AJ twirls to the center of the dance floor. She spreads her arms out and takes a bow. “Johann and I want to thank everyone for coming out today. It has meant so much to us to have all of our friends and family around for this festive day. Please drive safely for those that are heading home. For those that staying over, please walk safely to your rooms.” She chuckles. “Have a great night!”

People disperse to their vehicles and rooms, accordingly.

Chapter 15

Dark clouds slowly move across the sky. Fog starts rising up from the snow. The sun is hidden from sight. Thunder is off in the distance, but growing louder as it moves closer.

AJ stares out the window watching as this unfolds. She thinks to herself, "We had a wonderful Christmas eve and day. This storm rolling in, does this mean our visitors are leaving? I am not ready for them to go. I want another day with them."

Johann walks up to her and puts his hands around her shoulders. "I know what you are thinking and I am thinking the same thing. I wish we could have them around longer. However, that is selfish. They belong in their own time. I know they had a great time, but we cannot keep them. No matter how much we or they want to."

They stand silently in the window, continuing to watch the clouds and fog.

Both of them jump as the streaks of lightning light up the sky and the thunder cracks loudly. Looking at each other with wide eyes, they both sigh. "I wonder if that was the one where they leave us?" AJ asks.

"I don't know. We should go find out."

They open their bedroom door and Heinrich is standing there. Quickly they all embrace. Gustav walks up to them. "Wow! This storm is getting crazy. Do you think we'll be going back to where we started?"

"I'm not sure. We haven't figured out how it happens, but just that it does happen. We have the time hops and that includes the who, when, and where. No one has figured out the why, yet." Johann tells him.

The hallway fills with the time travelers. "Ok, let's all go to the kitchen for our day after Christmas leftovers for breakfast." AJ suggests. She motions for everyone to follow her.

As they walk to the kitchen, the rest of the family joins them. Carson moves to the front of the line by his mom, "Hey, are we having leftover treats along with the French toast?"

"Whatever is in the kitchen, is what we will have. I honestly, do not feel up to cooking. I can't wait for Mark to come back. He's a great caterer. His meals in my freezer are a lifesaver after the holidays."

Entering the kitchen, there's a shadow in the back corner. "Hello?" She questions.

"Hi! I'm Paul. Mark has sent me as your present to make you breakfast for the day after Christmas."

"Oh, Mark is so awesome. I seriously love this. We were planning on just warming up leftovers." AJ explains.

"Just for you, I am making your favorite breakfast. It's crepes with strawberry cream filling, paired with bacon and topped with whipped cream."

AJ looks up at Johann, "Did you know about this?"

"Nope, but I will certainly enjoy it with you. He makes everything yummy."

Cooper speaks up, "I am all in for crepes of any flavor."

"Of course you are." Carson laughs.

Everyone moves into the dining room as Paul brings out the food and places it around the table. There's no talking, just eating.

Minutes go by when Johann breaks the silence, "I think today will be a day for searching the internet to see if there's any update on how to get you all back to your own time. Trust me, it's not that we don't want you around, but we all need to be in our own place. Your place is back on the Kroonland so that you can see your family."

"We have all enjoyed our time hopping. It's been quite the adventure. Actually, the best adventure. I hope we will remember all of you and all of our travels." Gustav says.

Paul comes around picking up the empty plates. Cooper holds up his glass, "I want to give a toast to Mark and Paul for the great breakfast. I want to give a toast to our travelers. We love having you and learning from you."

They all raise their glasses and clank them together. AJ looks around the table smiling, "This is the best Christmas ever. I know, it's the day after, but that's ok. To me, it's the whole season. This year has been extra special with our guests here for Christmas. I wish you all safe travels back to 1903. For all of those that are from this current time, I wish you all a happy and prosperous year ahead."

There's a knock on the door. Johann starts to get up. Paul motions for him to sit and goes to answer it. "Merry Christmas! How may we help you?"

The voice on the other side replies, "We are here to surprise our parents."

Lizzie jumps up from table and runs to the door. She hugs her two boys. "Come on in. Come on in. Everyone will be excited to see you all."

Following behind her is Leo, Milo, and their spouses, Gabi and Mona. "Hey everyone! Look who has stopped by!"

"We figured it'd be a good idea to come over for a visit, being that everyone was here. We just got into town and will be here for a few days. Then we are back to South Carolina. It is way too cold and snowy here. I see some people that I don't recognize." Leo shares.

Axel stands up and gives them all a big hug, "I am so glad to see you all here. For our guests, let me introduce you to Leo and Milo. They are our boys and their wives, Gabi and Mona."

"Glad to meet you all. Let me introduce everyone. I am Heinrich. This is Gustav, my brother. Anton and Pauline, Ludwig and Julia, and Rudolfis and Karolina. They are fellow travelers. We were all on the Kroonland."

"So glad to meet you all. We have heard about most of you." Milo shakes their hands.

Paul inquires, "Are you staying in here or going to another room?"

"We will go into the living room. Come on, let's go." Johann motions. The friends get up and follow him.

The fire is crackling in the fireplace, everyone gathers around and sits. Johann says as he presses a button on the wall by the hearth, "My latest gadget is this new Surface Hub that comes down from the ceiling. I have put all of the time travel stuff in one folder. My favorite part is that I have all the pictures of every gathering that we have had throughout the years. Hopefully we can get some answers about how to get you all back to the Kroonland."

Thunder rolls through the castle and then lightning streaks across the sky among the dark clouds. It continues for a few minutes. It goes from streaks to being so bright that no one can see and then complete darkness.

The power is out and everyone is chattering. All the lights come back on as the generator kicks in. AJ looks around the room with a partial smile. “They must have all time hopped again. I wonder where they are now.”

“I don’t know, but hopefully they are safe.” Johann comments.

Chapter 16

Gustav opens his eyes to pure darkness. He reaches to his right and grabs an arm, “Heinrich, is that you?”

“Yes it is. Is there anyone else with us?” He inquires.

Anton answers, “We are here.”

“Us too.” Ludwig adds.

Rudolfis says, “Yes, we are here too. The next question is, where is here? I can’t see anything.”

“Total darkness at this point. Let’s feel around and figure it out. I don’t hear anyone else with us.” Heinrich tells the group.

Standing up, he feels the walls and finds a door. “I think we are back on the Kroonland. At least, it feels like it. Everyone, follow me.”

They each put a hand on the shoulder of the next one, and Heinrich guided them out of the room and onto the deck. As each one steps out into the bright moonlight, Ludwig excitedly proclaims, “We are back!”

“Ssshhhhh,” Julia hushes him. “You are going to wake the other passengers.”

"Do I see land?" Anton asks.

They all turn in the direction that he was facing. "Yes, that is land. I would say that we will be there in a few hours." Rudolfis answers.

The group walks over to the railing on the port side of the ship. Pauline's face lights up, "This sunrise is beautiful. Do you think we are back in our own time as well?"

"I do believe we are." Karolina replies.

Gustav looks over the bow of the ship and says, "I can see the Statue of Liberty. Also, a large building that appears to be floating in the water."

"That is Ellis Island. It's where we will be going." Heinrich informs him. "I heard that we dock across from it and then there are ferries that will be taking us over. We will all be examined and then on our way. Then we will catch the train to Saginaw, Michigan."

Anton inquires, "So, how long do you think it will take us to be on our way?"

"I have heard that it's normally three to five hours. That's if they don't find anything wrong. It'll be interesting to see how our group here will do, being that we've been time traveling. Hopefully we didn't pick up anything." Ludwig answers.

The group returns to their rooms to get all of their belongings. It takes minutes for Anton and Pauline to grab the bags that they ever unpacked.

A few moments later, Anton knocks on the door, "Heinrich, Gustav, are you guys ready? It's our turn to get in line."

Heinrich opens the door, "Yes, we are ready." He grabs his bag and Gustav follows behind him out into the hallway.

The four of them make their way up to the top deck finding the line is forming fast and the boat hasn't stopped yet. Stepping up behind the last person, Anton looking into Pauline's eyes, "This is our chance for a whole new life. I am excited to have this opportunity with you. Where do you want to go first?"

"I will to go wherever you go. Together we can go anywhere we want." She answers.

The line moves slowly. "I am glad to see that we go through all of this on the ship instead of on the island. This will get us on our way much quicker." Heinrich shares with them.

They get to the immigration official who verifies all the information that was on the ship's manifest. They all pass and move onto the next person that makes sure that they are all healthy enough to get off the ship and head for their final destinations.

An hour goes by and the group has passed all of their exams. "Now that we are done with that, let's go get our train tickets." Anton suggests.

Heinrich smiles and says, “We need to exchange our money before getting our train tickets.”

“That’s true. I forgot about that part.” Pauline responds.

Rudolfis walks up to the four-some. “Hey, everyone ready to get this adventure started? Karolina and I are.”

The group resoundingly replies with a YES! Picking up their bags, they walk to the exit ramp. There’s a voice behind that yells, “Heinrich!”

He turns around and yells back, “Ludwig! Julia! Are you joining us?”

“Yes we are. We can’t wait to get on that train.” Ludwig tells them.

As a full group of eight, they walk down the ramp to exit the ship, and stop at the money exchange window line. There are about a dozen couples ahead of them. They wait their turn and look around them.

Seagulls fly back and forth above them, landing on the light poles, and watching all the people.

“Can you believe all those buildings? This is a big city.” Gustav comments.

The clerk at the money exchange window yells, “Next!”

Heinrich and Gustav walk up first and convert their German marks for US dollars. Handing the money over, the clerk counts it, and gives them their new currency.

Next up is Anton and Pauline, followed by Ludwig and Julia, and the last of the group is Rudolfis and Karolina.

"Ready to go get our train tickets? Where is everyone headed? Gustav and I are headed to Saginaw, Michigan."

Anton replies, "Herminie, Pennsylvania."

"Cleveland, OH" Rudolfis answers.

Ludwig says, "Salt Lake City, Utah."

"Great. We'll be able to be on the train with each other for a bit." Heinrich tells them.

The pairs walk up to the train ticket window and each get the appropriate papers to get them to their destinations. They proceed to the train cars.

Frederick, the train conductor takes each person's ticket. "Welcome aboard. Enjoy your trip."

The ladies board first, finding their seats, and the men follow behind after passing off the luggage to the porter. The whistle blows and the train chugs forward out of the station as the black smoke trails along atop the windows.

"I know that we've said it before, but this is going to the best Christmas ever. The whole trip has been one adventure after another." Gustav says excitedly.

Pauline smiles and ponders, "My question is, should we be expecting to do more time traveling? If we do, will we continue where we left off? Will we see the great group of people who have been our hosts?"

"Excellent questions, however, I have no idea any of the answers. I wish we knew." Anton wraps his arm around her.

The group remains quiet for the next hour or more as they watch the landscape go past the window. Margarette, the lounge car attendant, walks up to their tables and asks, "What may I get you to drink?"

"We will each have a beer, what kind do you have?" Heinrich answers.

"We have Budweiser for this trip."

"We'll give that a try."

She steps to the next tables and takes their orders. Moments later she appears with everyone's beverages.

Ludwig announces, "I want to make a toast. Let's toast all of us travelers that have had a fun adventure thus far, and hopefully we will have lots more adventures in our new homes." The bottles clank together as they raise them.

The train clacks along out to the countryside. Trees line the tracks and the route is up and down hill until they get out into the mountains, where it is mainly back and forth to get up and over.

"This country is beautiful. I can't wait to see what it's like when we end up in Saginaw." Heinrich shares.

Looking out the window, Anton says, "We are almost to our destination. I am sad to say good-bye to all of you, but excited to see our family. They are never going to believe our journey to get here."

"I hear you. We've all become such great friends along this crazy adventure. We knew it was not going to be easy before starting out. However, one cannot expect to go time traveling." Gustav comments.

Frederick, the train conductor, comes walking through the car. "We will be pulling into Greensburgh within the next thirty minutes. Please get your things together and be ready to ready to disembark if this is your stop. For our next stop we will be heading northwest to Cleveland, Ohio. That portion of of our trip will take approximately eight hours."

Anton and Pauline gather their items together and give hugs to the rest of the group. "We will miss you all." She says fighting back tears.

As they pull into the station, they see the platforms and the rooftop of the station itself. The breaks are applied, and they slowly come to a stop. Passengers line up at the door and wave good-bye to those that are remain seated.

An hour passes with new people in the train car, and they hear the horn blow with the wheels starting to turn. This leg of their trip will take place during the night. The travelers sit back, close their eyes, and sleep for most of the time.

After a semi-rested slumber Heinrich opens his eyes, "Gustav, Rudolfis, Karolina, Ludwig, and Julia, you all need to wake up. Check out the sunrise over the trees. It's absolutely gorgeous!"

"Wow!" Karolina gasps.

Julia nods her head, "Yes! I love it!"

Fredrick returns, "Good morning everyone! We are getting close to Cleveland. You'll want to gather your things together and be ready for our next stop."

The train slows as it enters the large train station through one of its eight openings. When it stops, the passengers disembark. Rudolfis and Karolina give hugs before exiting.

"This is going to be a longer section. I hear it's over twelve hours." Gustav looks at Heinrich with concern.

"Yes, I have heard the same thing. This train ride is so long. I think what makes it feel even longer though is that we didn't have the long trip across the ocean. We cheated with having all the fun time travel adventures. I wonder if we could get transported to Saginaw instead of going by train the whole way." Heinrich laughs.

Ludwig chuckles, "If we had only figured that part out while we were traveling."

The group bursts out laughing and Frederick comes in and announces, "We are going to be having some great lake views for the first portion of our ride. Once we get into Michigan, we will be heading away from the water. This leg is much longer. We are going for over twelve hours. So, yes, that rumor is true. Sit back, relax, enjoy the first half, and then take a rest."

They get out a couple decks of cards to play poker to pass the time along. The sky gets dark, thunder cracks loudly, and lightning lights up the train car when in the next moment everything goes pitch black.

Chapter 17

Gustav opens his eyes and he can see nothing, not even his hand in front of his face. "Heinrich?"

"Yes, I am here. I cannot see anything either. Feel around you to find out where we are. I can feel the same chair that I was sitting in."

"That's what I feel as well." Gustav confirms.

Heinrich raises his voice and asks, "Hello? Anyone else here?"

There is no answer and no noises. It is completely dark and silent.

"I think we are alone. I am going to get up and see if I can find anything. This is weird. Normally when we time hopped we could see something when we got to our new destination." says Gustav.

He finds his way to the door and pries it open. The wind is fiercely blowing in his face. Shutting it he turns around, "I got nowhere with that. I guess I will just return to my seat."

"I thought that Ludwig and Julia were still with us. They should be on until we make the turn up to Michigan." Heinrich ponders.

The thunder rolls again and the lightning lights up the sky. They are blinded for a moment and their vision returns. Looking around they see the others on the train and can hear them talking.

Frederick comes up to their table, “Everything ok here?”

“Where are we? What happened?” Gustav questions.

He assures them, “There was a freak storm as we pulled out of Cleveland. Everything seems to be back to normal now. Sit back and enjoy the ride. We should be to Michigan in a few hours.”

Ludwig stops at with Julia, “We went for a brief walk into the next train car. Soon we should be getting some great views of the lake. They call it a great lake. We shall see what’s so great about it.”

“I heard that has to do with the size of the lakes.” Heinrich replies, “It was really weird with the storm that blew through. We thought we might be headed to another time hop.”

The couple sits down, and they all enjoy the scenery as it passes by.

Gustav remarks, “This lake looks huge. It looks more like an ocean than a lake. I guess that’s why they call it a great lake.”

“Yes, I agree. What I read is that this is not the biggest of the great lakes. So, if this looks this big, how big are the others?” Julia asks.

Heinrich answers, “You would be amazed how big they are. I read up on them. Lake Michigan and Lake Huron are technically one lake. They are separated by the straits of Mackinac. Then there is Lake Superior, which is the largest of them of all and it’s the deepest. There are some large freighters that sail on them. The smallest lake is Lake Ontario, which is the only lake that does not touch the state of Michigan.”

“I am impressed that you know so much about these lakes.” Ludwig comments.

“Thank you. I figured because we are going to Michigan that I should probably know something about the state. The lakes are interesting plus, the state is in the shape of a mitten. I am assuming that means it will be cold there.”

“Heinrich you are too funny.” Julia laughs.

Time appears to go by quickly while the four are playing poker. Frederick walks up, “How are we doing?”

“Great!” They all respond simultaneously.

“Glad to hear it. We are going to be pulling into Toledo within the next hour. You’ll want to get ready to head to your next destination. For Heinrich and Gustav going to Michigan, you can stay where you are. For Ludwig and Julia going to Salt Lake City, you will need to get on another train. It should say on your ticket which one.” He turns to the table next to them.

The four finish up the poker game and get their items ready for the next stop of the train. As they get close to the Toledo Union Station, there is a huge monstrosity of a building that comes into view.

"Look at that huge, ugly building. This is not the best building we have seen thus far." Julia comments.

Ludwig smiles, gives her a sideways hug, and replies, "This is true, but thankfully, this is not our last stop. Although the outside is ugly, maybe they have some good things on the inside. With the building being that large, I am sure there's a restaurant in there. They might have some good food."

"You are my positive thinker." She gives him a kiss on the cheek.

Coming to a complete stop, they all exchange hugs, and the couple exits onto the platform, waving as they walk away.

Heinrich and Gustav change seats to get by the window. A new pair sits down next to them. "Hi! My name is "Frank and this is my brother Kasper. We are on our way to a cute little town named Holly in Michigan. How about you two?"

"Glad to meet you both. I am Heinrich and this is my brother Gustav. We are going to Saginaw, Michigan." The men all shake hands.

Sitting back in their seats, Heinrich inquires, "Where have you two been? Is this part of a larger journey?"

"This is part of a much longer journey. We've been in America for a while." Grinning at Frank, "We have been on a lot of different journeys. How about you?"

"By different journeys, what do you mean?" Gustav asks.

Kasper hesitantly answers, "We aren't sure if you will believe us or not. Some people that we have talked to think we are crazy."

"Let me guess, you two have been time traveling or hopping." Heinrich tells him.

With shocked looks on their faces, they turn to each other and Frank questions, "How did you guess?"

"Gustav and I have been on quite a few time hops. We started out on the Kroonland ship and went on an adventure to the Edmund Fitzgerald in 1975, a lighthouse in Ludington, Michigan in 2001, then a castle in Rochester, Michigan in 2028. Next up we went to Frankenmuth, Michigan in 2035, and then to Wixom, Michigan in 2045. Our last stop before returning to our ship was back to the castle in Rochester, Michigan, but in the year 2050. It was all very crazy, but great."

Kasper nods, "We can relate, as we went to six time hops as well. We started out in New York. Our first stop was in Niagara Falls in 1975, followed by Louisville, Kentucky in 2001, and then Branson, Missouri in 2028. From there we went to Knoxville, Tennessee in 2035, on to Greenville, South Carolina in 2045. Our last time hop forward was to Frankenmuth, Michigan in 2050. This is where we ended up after that."

"It looks like if you start out in 1903, you go to the same years, even if you aren't going to the same places as others. We had some friends that went to Niagara Falls, New York in 1975 also. We wonder if we are in store for any more time hops or if this is it." Heinrich shares.

Frank responds, "I hope that we do have more time hops. We have seen some great things. It's a perfect way to see the country and what is coming down the timeline for us."

The train continues to clickity clack along the tracks as it makes it way through southeast Michigan. A few hours later Frederick walks into the car, "Hi everyone! We are getting close to the Holly Union Depot. This is a very small station. We only have a few of you disembarking. I love this little town. Please get your things together and be ready. This is a short stop."

As they round the bend, the small depot comes into view and the train slows to a stop. Kasper and Frank shake hands with Gustav and Heinrich when they get up from their seats to exit.

Within a view minutes the train is on its way and heading north. Heinrich and Gustav are alone at their table and playing cards once again to pass the time. It's dark outside and not much to see.

"We are in the final stretch. It appears we are on schedule. This is good because Karl should be waiting for us at the station when we get into Saginaw." Gustav thinks out loud.

Heinrich laughs, "Yes, It's less than a few hours. I am glad to be in this final stretch also. It will be interesting to see where we will be staying. Plus, we won't be moving."

The travelers close their eyes for what feels like a moment, and all of a sudden Frederick comes in announcing, "Attention passengers! We will be rounding the bend into the Potter Street Station in Saginaw, Michigan. I know that a lot of you are disembarking here. I hope that you have an awesome holiday season."

Grabbing their bags, they stand at the exit waiting for the train to come to a complete stop. Stepping off the car, Karl is waiting on the platform. The cousins embrace, as they haven't seen each other in months.

Karl says, "This is so exciting to see you both. You are going to love it here in Saginaw. You guys can stay with us until you can afford your own place. Let's go home and see everyone."

The men pile into Karl's brand-new model A car. Within a few minutes they are pulling up out front of his home where Albert and Rosa are waiting for them inside.

"Welcome!" They greet them as the men come into the house.

Albert says, "I hope your travels went well."

"We will get into all of that shortly. It went well, but it was full of way more adventure than what we had planned for." Heinrich shares with them.

Rosa motions for them to follow her, "Let me show you to your rooms."

"Thank you for your hospitality. We are tired from our long journey." Gustav tells her.

They follow her to the rooms, set the bags down, and lie on their own beds. Before long they are drifting off to sleep, and each of them are dreaming of the next adventures they will go on.

Character Profiles

Time Travelers

Heinrich Rindhage–He was born in 1874 in Germany and came to the USA in 1903 on the Kroonland. His brother, Gustav, joins him for this journey. He is 5' 6-½" tall and weighs in at 186 lbs. Heinrich served in the German Army for two yeas before coming to the USA. He is also the real great-grandfather to the author.

Gustav Rindhage–He was born in 1884 in Germany and came to the USA in 1903 on the Kroonland. He joined his brother, Heinrich, for this trip. Gustav is 5' 9" tall and weighs in at 175 lbs. He is the real 2nd Great Uncle to the author.

Anton Richter–He was born in 1866 in Germany and came to the USA in 1903 on the Kroonland with his wife, Pauline.

Pauline Richter–She was born in 1878 in Germany and came to the USA in 1903 on the Kroonland with her husband, Anton.

Ludwig Stein–He was born in 1863 in Germany and came to the USA in 1903 on the Kroonland with his wife, Julia.

Julia Stein–She was born in 1864 in Germany and came to the USA in 1903 on the Kroonland with her husband, Ludwig.

Rudolfis Kern–He was born in 1874 in Germany and came to the USA in 1903 on the Kroonland with his wife, Karolina.

Karolina Kern–She was born in 1876 in Germany and came to the USA in 1903 on the Kroonland with her husband, Rudolfis.

Frank Schönbaum – meets up with Heinrich and Gustav on the train. Brother to Kasper.

Kasper Schönbaum – meets up with Heinrich and Gustav on the train. Brother to Frank.

Friends of the Time Travelers

John–works on the Edmund Fitzgerald

William Robinson – lives in Ludington, Michigan with his wife, Margaret. Born in 1979

Margaret Robinson – lives in Ludington, Michigan with her husband, William. Born in 1980

Johann Reisender – lives in Rochester Castle with his wife, AJ. Brother to Carl and Kat. Born in 1986

AJ Reisender – lives in Rochester Castle with her husband, Johann. Mother to Carson and Cooper. Best friend is Vicki. Born in 1989

Carson Walker– married to Laila, son of AJ, and twin brother to Cooper. Born in 2013

Laila Walker – married to Carson. Born in 2015

Cooper Walker – married to Carla, son of AJ, and twin brother to Carson. Born in 2013

Carla Walker – married to Cooper. Born in 2014

Carl Reisender – Johann's brother, married to Anna. Born in 1984

Anna Reisender – married to Carl. Born in 1986

Eddie Laufer – lives in Wixom mansion with his wife, Kat. His best friend is Johann. Born in 1984

Kat Laufer – lives in Wixom mansion with her husband, Eddie. Johann's sister. Vicki is her best friend. Born in 1989

Vicki Haus – Kat's best friend. Married to Otis. Born in 1971

Otis Haus – married to Vicki. Born in 1968

Axel Krauss Sr. – married to Lizzie. Born in 1987

Lizzie Krauss – Eddie's sister. Married to Axel. Born in 1988

Leo Krauss – married to Gabi Krauss, son of Axel and Lizzie. Born in 2012

Milo Krauss – married to Mona Krauss, son of Axel and Lizzie. Born in 2015

Gabi Krauss – married to Leo Krauss. Born in 2013

Mona Krauss – married to Milo Krauss. Born in 2016

Burchard – Butler to Johann

Mark – Chef/Caterer for Johann

Paul – Works for Mark

Karl Kaldener – Cousin to Heinrich and Gustav. Lives in Saginaw. Born 1876. Arrived in the USA in 1903 on the Vaderland ship with Adolf.

Adolf Rheinhold – Cousin to Heinrich and Gustav. Lives in Saginaw. Born 1880. Arrived in the USA in 1903 on the Vaderland ship with Karl.

Albert Schlegel – Cousin to Karl and uncle to Adolf. Married to Rosa. Lives in Saginaw, Michigan.

Rosa Schlegel – Aunt to Adolf. Married to Albert. Lives in Saginaw, Michigan

Frederick – the train conductor

Places to Visit

The following places were mentioned in the story and are real locations that you can visit in person. They are all in Frankenmuth, Michigan.

Holz Brücke

Covered Bridge Ln.

frankenmuth.org/directory/holz-brücke-covered-bridge

This is a wooden bridge that is over the Cass River. There are walkways on each side of the bridge that are covered. This allows pedestrian traffic to cross safely.

Bavarian Inn Restaurant

713 S. Main St.

Bavarianinn.com

This is a restaurant famous for their family style chicken dinners.

River Place Shops

925 S. Main St.

Frankenmuthriverplace.com

Outdoor shopping in a Bavarian setting. The sidewalks are heated to make your year round shopping more enjoyable.

Places to visit continued

Bavarian Inn Lodge

1 Covered Bridge Ln.

Bavarianinn.com

Large hotel that includes a water park for family fun.

Bronner's CHRISTmas Wonderland

25 Christmas Ln.

Bronners.com

They are the world's largest Christmas store. This is located at the south end of town. They are open 361 days a year.

Silent Night Chapel

25 Christmas Ln.

Bronners.com

It is a replica of the original chapel in Oberndorf/ Salzburg, Austria. This is where the song "Silent Night" was sung on Christmas Eve in 1818.

About the Author

This is Mandy Jo's third published book. It's also the third genre that she has written in. This book was inspired by her love of genealogy. The main characters are based on and named for her great-grandfather and 2nd great-uncle. If you read Mandy Jo's first book, you may have recognized some of the characters in this story. There will be more books that include these characters.

Website - mandyjo.live

Twitter - @mandyjo_author

Facebook - @mandyjoauthor

Instagram - @mandyjo_author

Mandy Jo's Other Books

AJ is a divorced mother of twin boys. She has decided to get up off the couch and walk her first 5K. Follow her journey along the way.

The highlights of this book are the questions of walking your first 5K or to restart your walking journey are answered in story format. AJ and her ex get along and work together for the kids.

At the back of the book you will find her walking schedule, exercises, and places that she went to. Oh yeah, there are some recipes, but you'll love the comment at the bottom of them.

Available on Mandy Jo's website: mandyjo.live

Amaranth is born to an evil witch. However, her mother drops her off with a good witch and her family. She is raised in a good family environment.

One day her mother dies, word gets back to her, and then she is kidnapped. Amaranth finds out that it is her brother that orchestrated it. She does the unthinkable to escape.

Amaranth finds out who her father is and the whole sorted family tree.

This is the ultimate good vs evil. Which wins out in the end?

Does Amaranth go to the evil side or stay on the side of good?

Get your copy at mandyjo.live

More Books to Come!

2023

Mystery novel
Mystery/Paranormal
Fantasy
Time Travel

Yes, there are no exact dates or titles. You'll want to follow Mandy Jo on social media to find those out.